It was horrible watching Kris uncover the body, but what was even worse was wondering how he knew it was there...

I looked from Kris to the statue. "What are you doing?"

But he just carried on, apparently not caring about anything else. It was as if he was in a daze, unaware of what he was doing.

I stood there, completely still, then gently touched his arm. "Can we just go?"

Pushing my hand away, he continued scraping at the ugly statue in front of us. Kris had completely changed from being the lovely person I had known to someone totally different, someone evil. I was terrified. I didn't want to die, certainly not here, where I would never be found.

I stood there watching Kris, not saying a word. Then I started to scream, my body shaking. As the last piece of plaster fell from the head of the statue, I saw Jill's face staring back at me—two great big bloody holes where her eyes should have been, knife and bite marks all over her face.

Six friends go camping in the Cotswolds of England, not one of them realizing that death is just around the corner. They end up at an old house, seemingly empty, with a story attached to it—a story of a family's death. Friends together, just having fun...or so they think. One by one, they disappear. Only one survives to go into the witness protection program, depending on the police for survival. But who can she trust, when even the cops can be influenced by the evil within?

KUDOS for *Evil Within*

In *Evil Within* by Carrie Quesne, Carla Jenkins goes camping with five of her friends in the English country-side and winds up in an abandoned house. When her friends start disappearing and then dying, Carla is desperate to escape. But how can she leave her friends behind? And will just getting out of the house stop the carnage? Unfortunately for Carla, the answer to that last question is no, and she is forced to go into the witness protection program. But even then, she isn't safe. Strange things start happening after a while and, once again, the people close to her suffer. The story is chilling with a strong plot and good character development. You really feel for Carla as one thing after another goes wrong. ~ *Taylor Jones, Reviewer*

Evil Within by Carrie Quesne is the story of a psycho-pathic killer who targets a group of six friends on a weekend camping trip in England. Our heroine, Carla Jenkins, is the only one the six left to go into the witness protection program when the weekend is over. But even there she's in danger. Weird things begin to happen, and she feels someone watching her, so she knows the killer has found her and is just waiting for the right moment to strike. Now Carla is on the run again. Will she ever find a place where she can be safe and live a normal life? *Evil Within* is a complicated, intriguing mystery/suspense, short enough to read in one sitting, which is good because you won't be able to stop once you start. ~ *Regan Murphy, Reviwer*

EVIL

WITHIN

Carrie Quesne

A Black Opal Books Publication

GENRE: MYSTERY-DETECTIVE/THRILLER/WOMEN SLEUTHS

EVIL WITHIN
Copyright © 2017 by Carrie Quesne
Cover Design by Jackson Cover Design
All cover art copyright © 2017
All Rights Reserved
Print ISBN: 978-626945-90-6

First Publication: JANUARY 2017

Published by Black Opal Books **http://www.blackopalbooks.com**

DEDICATION

For my parents Mary and George
who believed in me from the beginning.

CHAPTER 1

Sitting here knowing what I know now, would I have gone with my friends that day? The answer? No way!

It was a cheery bright morning, that Saturday in September. My friends and I had planned a fun weekend out in the country, camping. *Camping!* I hated camping, but it was only for three nights. So, because of that, I didn't mind too much. Six of us were going—my best friend Lana with her on-off boyfriend Sam; Jill, whom I had known from infant's school; her boyfriend Max, whom I knew pretty well and who was a nice guy, especially to put up with Jill who was always trying to boss him around, but a lot of it was done jokingly. The main thing was they loved each other. Then, last of all, Kris. He was someone I had dated way back but only for a very short time. He had also gone to the same senior school as me. We hadn't seen each other for a long time. He had decided to move, and that was the last we saw of him, until now. He didn't tell us why he was back. I gathered he wanted to be near family.

Kris was tall, dark, and handsome with a fun, kind personality—always joking around, which I had loved about him.

Then there was me, Carla Jenkins. I was an only child, no siblings. I lived a fair distance away from my mother. My father had passed away a few years ago. My mother couldn't afford to live in a three-bedroom house and, not wanting to live in London any longer, had decided to move to Devon, to a quaint little seaside town called Dawlish. I knew she was happy there as she was near to my aunt, her sister. I visited my mother twice a year, and we phoned each other regularly. It suited me and kept my mother happy.

So that was all of us, all six of us, on the camping trip. But not six any longer, no longer…

಄಄಄

I was all packed and ready to go. We were taking two cars—Lana and Sam in one car with a lot of the cases and boxes of food. It was far too much stuff, really—

especially as it was only for a weekend. But Lana, along with Jill, had decided between themselves that we needed everything. It was fine with me, and no one else mentioned it. The rest of us were going in another car.

We were all so happy that day, singing silly little songs along the way. I sat in the back with Kris. He kept giving me quick little glances when he thought I wasn't looking. My stomach was doing somersaults, my hands all sweaty.

I kept thinking, *Stop being so silly, Carla, stop being so silly.* The thing was, I knew I was being all girlie, totally silly, and, really, I wasn't like that one bit. We were all driving out to a lovely part of the Cotswolds. I was certainly glad I was getting out of London for a while. I figured the others were, too. I had never been to the Cotswolds before but some of the others had. I knew it would take us at least a couple of hours to get there, so I'd made sure I packed a couple of books to take with me.

The drive went pretty uneventfully. We stopped twice, once at a petrol station to use the toilet and get something to eat. The second time we stopped was just off the road because Jill and Lana needed to go to the toilet again. This time they had to find some bushes and hearing them squeal was so funny.

Eventually, we arrived at our destination. It was a really pretty spot, and for the next three days it was going be all ours. There was a forest behind us and a lake in front. It was a beautiful blue lake which reminded me of a story I had read when I was young.

We had to drive down a dirt road to get there, as it was way out in the middle of nowhere. All I kept thinking was, *Will we ever get there?* The road seemed to go on and on, but we got there in the end. We all helped to unload everything, which didn't take too long.

Then the guys, with a little help from me, put up the tents. Lana and Sam had one tent, Jill and Max another, then the third tent was for Kris and me. I had said I would share one with him, especially as there was going to be plenty of room inside of it. Kris had his own sleeping bag and I had mine. I stood there, looking at the lake, knowing we were all going to have a fun time.

"Hey, Carla, snap out of it!" Lana shouted, "And come over here."

"I'm coming," I hollered, running over to them.

∽ఐ∽ఐ

We all sat around a log fire, eating hotdogs and telling silly stories. I sat right next to Kris and, somehow, his arm ended up around me, making me feel a little embarrassed, especially with everyone being there, but I was happy.

Getting ourselves ready for bed later, we were all about to retire to our tents when Max shouted for everyone to come and sit by the fire, which was starting to die down. There was a great big grin on his face, a really cheeky grin, which made me realize something was on his mind.

"I've got a bedtime story to tell you all," he said, the smile suddenly going away. "Are you sitting comfortably?"

We all shouted "Yes."

Max looked from one to the other of us. "Then I will begin, ladies and gentlemen. Not too far from here, I would say roughly an hour's drive away, is a great big empty house. It's totally empty. No one has lived in it for years. Seth Armstrong was the name of the gentleman who lived there with his wife Florrie. She was a beautiful woman whom all the men fancied. Over the years, they had four lovely children: three girls and one boy. The girls were as beautiful as their mother. The son took after his father—pretty plain, so they say. Well, that's what I was told."

"Wow," I whispered. "What happened?"

"I'm just getting to that bit," Max said. "Well, things gradually went from bad to worse. Seth got more and more jealous, thinking that his wife was having an affair. Not just that, but their son would go out with different girls every night and every time treat them really badly at the end of their dates."

Nasty man, I thought, as we all sat there listening to every word Max was saying.

"He beat a couple of the girls black and blue, one girl ending up in hospital. Anyway, one day Seth came home from work early and killed his wife and daughters, who were there with their mother at the time. When the police arrived, they just couldn't believe what they saw. It was a total blood bath."

"What about Seth?" someone asked.

"He was still there, covered in blood himself. The police arrested him. He's in prison."

Jill started to gag a little. "What happened to the brother?"

"No one knows, no one ever found him in the house. The police tried to find him but never could. Good riddance to him I say," Max whispered. "Good riddance."

He looked at each of us, in turn, with the great big grin back on his face.

When he turned to me, I looked him straight in the eyes. "You're makin it all up."

"No, it's all true...well, as far as I know, but I hope you all enjoyed your bedtime story."

As Kris turned to me, I suddenly felt very nervous, like a little school kid again. Right then, I wished he wasn't there as I hated feeling that way. I knew I was being silly. He took hold of my hand, leading me to our tent.

I wanted to be with him but, at the same time, he scared me—the whole situation scared me.

We all said our goodnights to each other then settled down to sleep.

ເ໑ເ໑

The next day, all of us got up nice and early. The sun was already trying to get through the clouds. I knew it was going to be a fun day for us all. We sat looking toward the sky with smiles on our faces. We were all glad that we had decided to go on the weekend campout.

I knew the guys were really happy because they always loved going camping, but they were very surprised about us girls, especially me, knowing how much I hated it. The guys made a fire and the girls, mainly me and Lana, made breakfast.

"Yummy, eggs and bacon!" shouted Sam and Kris together, making us all laugh.

After breakfast, we all went down to the lake for a swim and, off course, a wash. It was chilly this time of day but we got used to it in the end, especially the guys. Nothing seemed to faze them. After we had dried off and changed clothes, Max started pacing around. He had that great big smile on his face again. Bless Max. He was always the happy, optimistic guy who Jill had fallen in love with. "Hey, everyone, I know what we can do," he shouted, making everyone laugh.

"Oh? What?" Jill yelled back. "What's that? Is it something exciting? Max, don't make us beg."

Poor Max couldn't get a word in it. Jill wasn't giving him chance to say what he wanted to. I gave her one of my stern looks as she was just about to say something else. That was all she needed and not another sound came from her mouth. We all glanced at Max, letting him know that he could continue.

"Are you ready to listen to me now? Okay, good. I shall carry on. You know what we should do? I think we should all go up to the house."

"Whose house?" I asked.

"Seth Armstrong's house. Whose do you think?"

"Great idea," someone agreed. "Let's do it."

I turned. It was Kris. He had spoken so softly I hadn't realized it was him. As I looked at him, he gave me a lovely smile which made me go all goose bumpy inside. I smiled back at him, not knowing what else to do.

We all sat for a short while, debating what we should do and whether going to the house was the right thing or not. Everyone decided that, yes, it was—apart from me, and I knew I was just being a coward. Worst thing was, though, they decided that later in the afternoon would be the best time to go, the later the better.

We spent most of our time sunbathing, swimming, and playing volleyball: girls against the boys! Us girls won, which didn't go down too well with the guys. We ate our lunch of was cold chicken salad and potatoes and, throughout the day, the guys drank beer or coke.

We girls were drinking lemonade and Pepsi, except for Lana, who had one or two beers. Trust Lana. She always had to be one of the guys, or at least she thought she did. She was certainly a tomboy at times and had been when we were at school.

I remembered her going to school in trousers one day, which didn't go over too well with the teachers.

She was made to write on a full sheet of paper *I won't come in trousers again*, line after line, filling the whole page.

CHAPTER 2

Late afternoon arrived a little too quickly for me. After putting our things away in the tents, making sure everything was safe, we got into our cars, ready to leave. I didn't know for sure, but I thought everyone was feeling a little apprehensive about going. But no one said a word.

It was just some empty old house we were going to, so, really, no big deal. The thing was it was a big deal, especially to me, and I didn't know why. I wasn't scared of anything...well not much, or at least nothing that I couldn't see and certainly nothing that went bump in the night.

Max drove, with me, Kris, and Jill. He claimed he knew the way, so Lana and Sam followed in their car. We drove fairly slowly, as it was pretty much all dirt roads and lots of winding lanes, just barely wide enough for one car. We were all pretty quiet most of the time, which pleased me, as I really didn't feel like talking. Every so often, I could sense Kris looking at me, but I never glanced his way.

Eventually, we came to two giant gates which looked old and rusted. They had certainly seen better days. Driving through them, we went down a lane that seemed to go on forever.

Then, all of a sudden, there it was in front of us, standing there, all huge and sombre, looking so dark and eerie, and kind of sad.

We stopped, parking right near the house. Right then, I knew I didn't want to be there, certainly not to go inside. Something in me said, *Don't go in there, Carla, don't go inside that place.*

All of the others seemed so excited, but as I looked at Kris, I noticed apprehension—or was it terror I saw in his face? It only lasted a few seconds, but that was all I needed to realize that something was wrong, something was bugging him, and I had no idea what. Kris came over to me, took my hand, and, together, we followed the others inside.

"It's huge," someone whispered.

"I totally agree with you." And I did. It was too big for my liking.

"You mean cold," Lana said in a sing-song voice.

"It's both of those," I said, though I knew no one but Kris was listening to me.

I looked at him with a half-smile on my face. He smiled back at me. As we all made our way into the living room, all I wanted to do was turn around and run away. I didn't feel right. Everything about the whole situation seemed wrong. I glanced at everyone and decided maybe it was my imagination running wild.

Someone made a remark about the lounge as we went in. It was the biggest room for a lounge I had ever seen. I had seen quite a few sitting rooms in my time, but this was by far the biggest of them all. It was full of quaint old furniture, mostly antique, with a beautiful stone fireplace.

Someone certainly knew how to decorate and make something look beautiful.

Sam and Kris went over to the fireplace, where they began to light the fire for us. It was welcomed by all of us. Everywhere just felt cold and smelled musty and damp. Within a few minutes, we had a warm fire blazing away, which we were all very grateful for. I looked at Sam and Max. Both of them were babbling on about something. I really didn't know what. I felt far away, as if I was in a dream.

Everyone in the room, apart from me, was laughing. I guessed it must have been one of Sam's jokes, as they all seemed to be staring at him. Out of everyone, Sam was the joker. Sometimes they were funny jokes, other times not so funny, even though everyone always laughed at the end of them.

"Carla, Carla! wakey-wakey," someone shouted at me, which brought me back to the here and now.

Looking up, I saw it was Lana. She had a great big smile on her face, which cheered me up no end. Lana, from the very first time I had met her, always could lift my spirits. I remembered feeling so alone at school until Lana moved with her family to our area, ending up at my school, becoming my best friend. Just seeing her smiling face every day at school helped me through my hardest times. She was also there for me when I was twenty years old and my dad died. I owed her everything.

"I'm fine, thank you," I almost whispered.

"Your welcome," she said as she hurriedly got up and came over to me, putting her hand in mine.

I sat there, right next to Lana, wondering why I was feeling so low, eventually putting it down to the sombre, eerie, scary place.

Yes, it was all of those. I wished I could feel as cheerful as the others. Though, glancing from one to the other, I wondered if they truly felt as cheerful as they looked. Yes, this place scared me. There was something about the house, almost as if it was alive. Maybe it *was* alive and telling us to leave.

"Sorry, Lana." I was. I didn't want to spoil anything for anyone.

"Let's have some fun, everyone," Max said.

We all smiled and shouted out, "Okay" in unison, which made us all laugh.

Right then, we should have left. The biggest mistake we made was to stay.

All of us...well, maybe not me, finally decided we should have a look around and see what we could find. Kris and I ended up together, which of course I didn't mind. I liked him, or maybe it was a little more than like. We all decided an hour would be good, and then we were to meet back in the lounge, which everyone agreed to. Kris took my hand and, as I took the torch in my other hand, my thoughts were on him. Right then, nothing else mattered. Standing there, I noticed my hand was shaking. The torch was going up and down.

Oh, you stupid thing. Calm down, girl.

Kris gently took the torch from me, and we slowly walked, hand in hand, along a corridor which had great big statues on either side of it. The statues were of ugly, deformed birds or creatures. I wasn't quite sure what they were, and Kris, when I asked him what he thought they might be, just shook his head, telling me he had no idea either.

All I knew was that they scared me silly. They made me feel cold and shivery inside. Down at the end of the

corridor, we came to a great big door, a door which so
was big and ugly that I almost turned around and ran to
safety, scared of what we would likely find on the other
side.

I knew Kris was going to take me into the room on
the other side of the door, but I didn't want to go, not
even with him. I was so frightened, but about what, I had
no idea. Kris slowly opened the door. It was big and
heavy and made an awful squealing noise as it opened.
As he walked inside, I followed him, staying as close to
him as possible. I was so relieved when I saw that it was
only a kitchen. It was a huge room, almost as big as the
lounge, but nothing more than a kitchen. It had two old-
fashioned butler sinks, a very large AGA range, and an
American-sized refrigerator.

In the middle of the room was a huge oak table, big
enough to seat at least eight people if not more, and at
one end of the room was a glass door that led into a large
greenhouse. It was full of plants and flowers of every
kind. I noticed they were all in bloom. How could they
be? The house was empty and had been for a long time.
They should have withered and died. I called Kris over to
me, and he seemed almost surprised as me. His theory
was that maybe there was a relative or friend looking after the place, especially in the greenhouse. So I went
along with what he said, thinking how plausible it sounded.

The next room we went into was a library, full from top to bottom with books, but what caught my eye was a great big old fireplace. The patterns around it were beautiful, all done in what looked like silver and gold. There were some cute little cherubs above the mantel piece and, right on the mantle in the very middle, a lovely old clock. It was a comfortable room with two big worn armchairs.

I noticed Kris was sitting in one of the chairs and—for just a second, only one split second—it seemed like he totally belonged there. He was grinning at me in such a strange way, it made me feel very uncomfortable. I wanted to turn and run. I slowly started to walk out of the room.

"Hey, wait!" Kris shouted at me, making me jump. "Wait for me, girl."

We decided to go and wait for the others in the sitting room. I was very grateful that he agreed with me, feeling nervous as I was. I was also thankful that he never mentioned looking upstairs. No way did I want to venture any farther. I was a scaredy cat, frightened of what we would find. When we got to the sitting room, it was totally empty. So we just sat by the fire, waiting for the others to return.

Kris chatted on about work and what he had done a week ago on the weekend.

"…it was the best party ever," I heard him say, but to tell the truth I was only half listening to him. "Carla, are you awake? Carla!" he shouted at me. "Wake up, sleepy-head."

Looking at Kris with his happy, smiley face, I burst out laughing, knowing how hollow it sounded, certainly to me, but hopefully not to Kris.

"Where were you, sleepy head? Carla, are you okay?"

"I'm fine." It wasn't true but I couldn't tell him that. "I'm good, so please stop asking me, Kris, okay?"

"Okey dokey."

We sat in silence as we waited for the others to return and, eventually, Lana and Sam came in, but no Jill and Max. While we were waiting for the others, we talked about what we had seen and the rooms we had been in. I told them that Kris and I had found the kitchen which had led to a greenhouse, full of beautiful plants and flowers, all in bloom.

"What do you mean all in bloom?" Sam asked."

"We think someone is looking after them," I said as quietly as I could.

"Wow! That's amazing," Lana blurted out, laughing.

We all sat quietly, not really knowing what to say to each other until Lana started singing. Lana, bless her. She loved to sing but didn't have the best of voices. But right then, I welcomed her singing and was so glad she was in the room with us. I loved her dearly. She was such a wonderful friend.

We were all starting to worry about Jill and Max. I stood and started to pace up and down, to the discomfort of everyone else. I could tell by their faces that they wanted me to stop and sit down. I was feeling very on edge, and I knew the others were too. I went over to the window. I noticed one of the cars had gone and called to the others to come over and see. They rushed to where I stood, looking out the window.

"Look out there," I shouted, pointing outside. "They've gone back to camp."

I really didn't know what to think. One thing I did know for certain, Jill wouldn't just go off like that.

"But why not tell us?" Lana said, nearly shouting in my ear. "Why haven't they told us?"

"It was strange that they never said anything to any of us, I realize that," Kris said in an authoritative voice. "But maybe they wanted to go off quickly and couldn't find any of us."

I knew he was wrong but I didn't say so. There was no point. We couldn't do anything.

"They didn't look hard enough then," Lana mumbled to herself.

I was pretty certain by then that everyone was feeling a bit pissed off and, as I looked at Kris, there was anger in his face, which scared me. Luckily, it just lasted a few seconds but a few seconds was enough for me to realize he didn't seem like the Kris I had once known.

We all made our way to the car to go back to camp. I was so grateful to be out of the house, I felt like a weight had been lifted off me. We were about to get into the car when Sam called for us to stop and pointed to the tires. We all gasped. Someone had slashed our tires and covered the side of the car with what looked like black paint. There were scratch marks all over it. The tires were ruined and, as Kris looked in the boot for the spare tire, it was ruined too. We certainly were not going anywhere, not unless we could get help. Tears came to my eyes. Going back inside was the last place I wanted to be. I knew the house didn't want us back. It was telling us to stay out, but we didn't listen.

We slowly made our way back inside and straight to the sitting room where the fire was still blazing away. I sat down slowly, so wanting to turn and flee, but there was nowhere to run to. I felt like bursting into tears just as Lana came over to me and took hold of my hand, letting me know things would be all right. But things would never be all right again. Something bad was happening. Everywhere stank of death. I was really scared and, even though the others didn't say much, I thought they were just as scared as me. I turned to Lana then to the others, trying to smile, but it didn't turn out to be the smile I wanted it to be. It wasn't even half a smile. I knew I was putting extra dampers on things but, right then, I didn't care.

Kris came and sat next to me, looking at all of us, one by one. "I think something might have happened to Max and Jill, after all."

"Stop fooling around, don't try and scare us, Kris," Lana said with a tremor in her voice.

"Kris, please don't," I agreed.

He turned to me, his face solemn, his eyes telling me to be quiet. "I'm not fooling around. Something has happened. Nothing feels right."

I knew what he meant. I felt just like he did.

"Please don't, do—" Lana couldn't finish speaking she was so upset.

"Stop trying to scare us, you guys. We're scared enough," I butted in, wanting them to know how Lana and I felt.

"I think he may be right," Sam almost whispered. "I feel the same as Kris right now. We have to do something to find them, even if, in the end, they happen to have gone, after all."

I could tell Lana was upset, even though she wasn't allowing her emotions to show. I was the one out of the two of us who usually never allowed my emotions to erupt, but deep down all I wanted to do was run away as far away as possible.

I felt like screaming but it would be pointless. It would just make matters worse than what they were. There was no one to help us. We were by ourselves. So many emotions inside of me were desperate to come out, and they were coming out little by little, much to my disgust. Looking around at Lana, I knew I had to be strong.

I put my arm around her, and we sat there quietly together. Silence. It was the total silence I could not bear, but it was all around us, and there was nothing we could do. I didn't know how long it was—seemed like hours—until someone spoke. It must have only been a short time, really.

Sam stood. "I think Kris and I should go and try to find Max and Jill."

I didn't want them to leave us, but I knew someone had to try, even if we found out they were not in the house, after all. Something inside of me said they were still in the house. Alive or dead, I truly had no idea. *Alive, dead?*

I didn't want to think about it because my thoughts always came back to dead. My feelings were so strong that I was sick to my stomach. Sitting with Lana, I had to be strong for her, even though I didn't feel up to it.

I just wanted to turn and run out of that evil place and not stop until I finally got to safety.

いのい

The guys had been gone a good while by then, and I was starting to get pretty worried about them, and about

Lana and myself. Not knowing what to do, I turned to Lana. "We'll give them another half an hour."

Lana and I were so tired but I knew we would never be able to sleep. I was really frightened that if we did fall asleep, we would never wake up again.

"Carla, what if they don't come back? What if it's only you and me?"

"Don't, Lana. It'll be good. Everything's going to be all right." I knew it wasn't. Death was all around. "We'll go and look for them, so don't worry." I tried to be as gentle with her as I possibly could. "It will be okay," I repeated, almost to myself.

Fifteen minutes slowly went by, the slowest fifteen minutes ever for me. I was just about to get up when we heard someone shouting. We had no idea where it was coming from, as it sounded like it was coming from a distance away. As we both jumped up, I took hold of Lana's hand and was just about to move when we heard the most hideous, horrendous noise I had ever heard in my life. Lana gripped my hand tightly, so tight I thought she was going to break the bones in it.

It almost sounded like someone was being strangled, then we heard an awful gurgling sound, and someone somewhere started screaming out the most obscene language we had ever heard. Even being a distance away, we could hear almost everything, although I wished we couldn't, because I knew that it would stay with me forever. Lana started to cry, which turned into heart-wrenching sobs. I felt like crying too but I had to be strong for the both of us. I knew she was petrified because I felt the same way.

"Oh, Carla, please let's leave, please let's leave. I don't like it."

"Shush, darling, it's going to be all right." I tried to comfort her but how could I when I felt the same? So all I did was put my arms around her, holding her tight. "Hush, hush, Lana, I won't let anyone harm you. I will take care of the both of us."

"Carla—"

"You needn't say anything, Lana. We'll be all right, darling." My heart was beating so fast I thought it would burst.

More than anything, I wanted to get out of the house, but where we would go, how far would we get without a car?

CHAPTER 3

We sat in silence. It was deathly quiet now.

"We can't go anywhere, Lana, we have no car. There's nowhere to go. We have to wait until morning, then maybe—"

"If we survive until then!" she screamed at me.

And she was right. We might never survive this horrendous ordeal, something I didn't want to think about, as I always ended up with one word in my mind, death. One thing I did know for certain, I wasn't going to wait around and do nothing.

"I think we should go and look for the guys," I told Lana, knowing deep down inside of me they were probably dead. The thought made me shudder.

"You stupid, stupid fool. You know they're dead.

We'll never find them. We're next. We're going to die, both of us, Carla."

She started hitting me, as if she was possessed. I hurt for my friend but knew that anything that I said wouldn't be heard. She was too scared to listen to me.

I took hold of her hands. "Sit quietly and wait for me."

But, looking at her, I knew exactly what she was thinking. I noticed her shudder as I spoke to her. I didn't want to leave her but I had to. I had to at least try and find our friends. As I moved toward the door, a small, faint voice told me not to go. but the stronger part of me said *You must, you must go*.

I turned to Lana and, going back to her, I led her to a hidden spot behind the couch covering her with cushions. "I want you to stay put, dearest friend, until I get back."

She was totally silent, which scared me, but I had to go. Kissing her on the forehead, I walked out the room, not turning back, knowing if I turned around, I would go and hide with Lana.

"Oh, Lana, I want to hide with you," I muttered under my breath. I did, I wanted to turn around and hide with her.

Closing the door behind me, I quickly hurried out of the room and started to walk down the long corridor with all the ugly, disgusting looking deformed statues on either side. I stopped to look at one of them. "Gargoyles, that's what they remind me of!" I knew what gargoyles looked like, as I had seen pictures of them in magazines.

Shivering, and not because of the cold, but from the evil stench of the house, which was all around me, I carried on searching. I approached the kitchen door. It took all my strength to open it. Going inside, I hurried to the cabinet, where I took out a long sharp knife, the sharpest I could find. Feeling a little bit better holding the knife, I walked out of the kitchen, I was just about to start searching again, when I heard Lana screaming for help. Then I heard the most hideous laugh. I had never heard anything so horrendous in my life. Someone was trying to hurt my friend.

I found I couldn't move. I wanted to help her, needed to help her, but was rooted to the spot. Tears started falling and suddenly something inside of me snapped. My feet finally moved, and I ran as fast as I could to the sitting room. My heart was beating so fast I thought it would explode. Just for one tiny second, I stopped outside the sitting room door. For that second, time stood still then, snapping myself out of it, I rushed inside. Everything that was in the room had been smashed to bits.

"Lana, Lana." She had gone. "Oh, Lana, I am so sorry, so sorry, what have I done?" I whispered.

Standing there, shaking like a leaf, I felt so helpless. I didn't know what to do. Lana had gone like the others. It was all my fault. I should never have left her. Feeling as guilty as hell, I started to scream and shout, wanting to cry but, if I did, I might never stop.

"Come on, you stupid son of a bitch, come and get me if you dare. Come and get me." This time, I screamed it out, knowing no one was listening but it was making me feel a tiny bit better.

Suddenly, the reality of it all struck me. They were gone, all gone, apart from me. I felt so scared and alone, knowing that I would be next. Looking at my watch, I saw that was four p.m. I was totally exhausted so, sitting down, I laid my head back and closed my eyes, waiting for my fate.

The silence was agonisingly cruel, but I never moved. I didn't dare.

Sometime later, I felt someone touch my arm, making me scream. Jumping up, about to slash with the knife, I heard a voice shout for me to stop. I turned around, only to face Kris. Dropping the knife, I rushed into his arms, nearly knocking him over.

"Kris," I sobbed, "where have you been? I thought you were dead. They're all gone, all gone. There's no one left, apart from you and me."

"Sam was in one room, and I went off to look in another one," he told me as we sat together. "But when I went back to the room Sam had been in, he wasn't there. I searched everywhere for him, but I couldn't find him so I finally decided to come back to the sitting room. I found a door which led down to the cellar. There were even more rooms down there but no one else." He took hold of my hand. "Come, Carla let me show you."

I stood up. "Did you hear anyone screaming or any horrible noises?"

"No, I didn't hear anything."

The look Kris gave me was of pure hatred. It lasted just one tiny second—enough for me to realize something wasn't right. Kris had changed from Mr. Nice Guy to someone I wanted to be far away from. I felt cold and something deep inside of me said *Don't go, get away from him, and run.*

I dropped my hand to my side and moved away from him, wanting to turn and run. His face was totally empty of emotion. I couldn't tell what he was thinking and that scared me. I was so frightened all I kept thinking of was that it must be Kris. Kris was the killer.

"Kris—"

"No, Carla, it's not me" he butted in. "I know you think it is. Carla, don't look at me that way. I won't hurt you, babe."

"Please stay away, don't touch me," I told him, trembling.

"Carla girl, Carla."

I so wanted to trust him, I desperately needed someone to help me get away from this evil place, away from this house of death. I didn't know what to do. I felt so scared and alone, fearing my fate was sealed. What could I say to him? But I didn't get the chance to do or say anything.

Kris suddenly heaved a sigh. "I need to talk to you, but only when we're out of the awful situation we're in."

I looked at him then at the door and, before I could do anything, he took hold of my hand.

"I love you so much, Carla."

I didn't know what to think. My head was spinning. I thought I was going to faint. Did I trust Kris? For one tiny, tiny second, yes came into my head. Then I looked at him again and something once again snapped inside of me. I had to get away from him. Fast. I pulled my hand from his and backed away from him.

"I've been trying my mobile all night, Carla, but nothing. What about you?"

"Same here," I blurted. "Nothing."

Kris took my hand again, holding it so tight I thought he was going to break it. Almost dragging me out of the sitting room, he turned and gave me a quick peck on the cheek.

I quickly moved away from him. "I forgot my handbag."

"Hurry up now, my sweetest, don't be long," he drawled. "Kris doesn't like to be kept waiting."

The way he spoke to me scared the hell out of me, but I knew if I didn't go with him, he would come and get me, so I grabbed my bag and rushed back to him, tears in my eyes. Kris was a short distance away, staring at one of the statues. I should have run but my feet wouldn't move. I felt as cold as ice. Tears ran down my face—tears of desperation, tears of terror for the fate that was in store for me. For no reason, he started scraping away at the head of the statue with some sort of pocket knife. Bits of plaster or wax dropped onto the floor.

I looked from Kris to the statue. "What are you doing?"

But he just carried on, apparently not caring about anything else. It was as if he was in a daze, unaware of what he was doing.

I stood there, completely still, then gently touched his arm. "Can we just go?"

Pushing my hand away, he continued scraping at the ugly statue in front of us. Kris had completely changed from being the lovely person I had known to someone totally different, someone evil. I was terrified. I didn't want to die, certainly not here, where I would never be found.

I stood there watching Kris, not saying a word. Then I started to scream, my body shaking. As the last piece of plaster fell from the head of the statue, I saw Jill's face staring back at me—two great big bloody holes where her eyes should have been, knife and bite marks all over her face.

CHAPTER 4

Tears streamed down my cheeks.

Kris turned to me and held me gently in his arms until I had calmed down. Stepping away from me, he stood looking at me with pity in his eyes. "It's going to be all right, my darling." The way he said my darling, the way he spoke, scared me.

I suddenly realized how calm he was with everything, especially seeing Jill's face. It had to be Kris. No way would someone sane act like he was now. Kris was the killer. How, I really had no idea. How did he do it when it would have taken time? He just never had time, as he was usually with someone.

An awful thought came to me. Where was the rest of Jill? Then I started to gag, wanting to throw up. I couldn't stop myself. I started vomiting. Everything that was in my stomach came out and, when I had finished being sick, I felt so exhausted I just slumped onto the floor.

"Carla girl, I have something special to show you, come along."

My whole body felt like lead. I was totally numb all over.

"I can't move," I whimpered.

"Don't say 'can't,' Carla girl."

I hated the way he called me Carla girl, hated the way he said it. I knew I had to go with him because then I just might have a slight chance of getting away. So I followed him down a long corridor, passing more of the hideous statues, wondering what lay underneath them. I shuddered suddenly as horrible thoughts of who might be under the rest of them came into my head.

Turning, he took my hand, squeezing too tightly, but I stayed quiet, not saying a word, hardly daring to breathe. Finally, we came to a door. It made an awful screeching sound as Kris started to open it. It was another giant of a door, huge and ugly looking and stank of death. He started to drag me through it and down some steep steps. I felt almost paralysed. My feet wouldn't move.

Kris dragged me from step to step, clearly not caring if he was hurting me or not. As we got near to the bottom I tried to pull my hand away but it made him hold even tighter, hurting me more. I was scared to death of him right then, scared to death of the whole situation. The change in him from sweet and gentle Kris to what he was now made me realize that death was just around the corner for me.

"Oh, Kris, why are you doing this, why?" I whispered through a throat so tight my words were barely loud enough for him to hear.

"I think you know the answer to that, my dearest one," he spat, out almost screaming at me. His voice sent shivers down my spine.

"I don't understand, Kris," I whimpered.

"Hello, my little sister, here she is."

I turned to see who he was talking to. Right there in front of me was a girl, and although I couldn't see her face properly, I guessed she was quite young. Her hair was long, almost covering her face, and her finger nails were ripped, and bloody. She was filthy, as if she hadn't washed for weeks, maybe even months. The smell coming from her was so bad that I almost gagged. The awful creature was pregnant, so she must have been older than I first thought. I stared at Kris then at the girl. Both of their faces were pure evil. I started to scream and couldn't stop.

Faintly and as if from far away I heard a voice saying, "Make her shut up. Kill the slut, kill the slut."

Kris slapped me hard across my face.

"Again, again. Kill the bitch," the girl screamed.

As he slammed his fist into my face, I thought I was going to die. Everything started spinning in front of me, and then there was nothing but darkness.

CHAPTER 5

When I awoke. I found I couldn't move. At first, with all my grogginess, I thought I was just temporarily numb, but then realized I was tied to some sort of chair. What I could see of it, which wasn't much, reminded me of a dentist chair. Trying to look around as best as I could, I noticed to the right of me there was a high table with what looked like some sort of surgical stuff on it. Syringes and something that looked like a mask, one that people used to wear in the war. Worst of all, in the center of the table, was a knife. As my eyes focused, I saw it was more than just a knife. It was a doctor's scalpel. My heart started to pound so badly I couldn't breathe, I tried to move but couldn't. My face was hurting from where Kris had struck me, and my mouth was bleeding. But I couldn't do anything about it. I knew I was going to die. Maybe that would have been the best thing to happen to me, better than what lay ahead.

I was a great big coward when it came to pain. Someone just had to pinch me and I would scream, so I was terrified of what I imagined was to come. Death would be the best way out, and only a quick death would do.

Right then, it was death or a miracle.

Suddenly, someone entered the room but I couldn't see who it was. I was petrified. I knew my fate was sealed. I was going to die. I shut my eyes, praying it would be a quick death with no pain. Tears started to fall.

"Carla, it's me. Shush."

"Lana, is that you?"

"Yes, now be quiet."

"Thank God, you're alive." I almost shouted for joy but Lana quickly covered my mouth.

"Shush, not now. Later, when we get out of here."

Slicing at the ropes, she finally cut the last one off me. Leaping quickly out of the chair, which made me shiver just looking at the thing, I hurried out of the room after Lana. We made our way to the stairs, both of us praying out loud that Kris and that sister of his wouldn't turn up. As Lana put her foot on the first step of the stairs, we heard a noise from one of the rooms close by. It was very faint and, at first, I thought I had imagined it. All I wanted to do was continue up the stairs and get out of the house as quickly as possible, and I was sure Lana felt the same. We both knew that if we didn't get out right away, we might never get out alive. Looking at Lana, though, I could see she was as frightened as I was. But I had to see were the sound was coming from. It could be our friends.

As I turned to go, Lana grabbed me and, with tears in her eyes, begged me not to leave. "Carla, please don't, I don't want to die, not here."

"We won't, that I promise you, sweetheart. We have to do this. You know we have to."

"Yes, we have to. I know that, but—"

"We will be okay, Lana, I promise."

"Okay, please, let's hurry."

Hand in hand, we slowly made our way to where we heard the strange noises coming from. The door was slightly open. We inched our way in, as quiet as two mice. I was stunned. There, in front of us, was the most horrific sight we had ever seen, ever wanted to see. Four tables were in the room. They looked like operating tables that you'd see in hospitals, and on two of them were two people.

As we got a little closer, Lana let out a small scream, Sam and Max lay on the tables—not that there was much left of them. I noticed that Sam's head was almost hanging off his neck and there were great big deep bloody gashes across his chest. Blood was everywhere. I wanted to turn and run but something stopped me.

Max—what was left of *him*—lay on the other table. As we stared, both of us started to gag at the same time. Our vomit joined the blood on the floor. He had no arms and one of his legs was sliced right through up to his groin. Tourniquets had been applied to his stumps and at the top of his leg to stop the worst of the bleeding, probably so he wouldn't die too quickly. Staggering backward, I grabbed Lana just in time, as she fell to the floor. Kneeling down, I held her in my arms, trying my best to comfort her, wanting to be comforted myself. As we stood to move, we heard a gurgling sound. It was coming from Max. He was still alive, but only just.

As I stood there, staring, not knowing what to do, Lana jerked my arm. Taking her hand, knowing there was nothing we could do, I ran out of the room with her. Just as we were about to go up the stairs, the cellar door slowly opened, making that awful screeching sound. I shuddered.

I grabbed Lana and shoved her under the stairs, the only hiding place I could see. I slid in beside her and prayed for help as we stood there in silence. Heavy footsteps came down the stairs, and I could hear Kris telling his sister something, but I couldn't understand what was said. As they headed down the corridor, we quickly and quietly made our way up and out of the cellar. Then, hand-in-hand, we ran. Coming to the front door, we shoved it open together and ran outside, finally breathing in the fresh air. I nearly shouted for joy.

"Carla, what now? What shall we do?"

"Run and don't stop." All I wanted was to be away from the house, the house of death. "Just run, Lana."

Suddenly, we heard the loudest, most bloodcurdling screams coming from inside the house. Looking at each other, we started to run. We hadn't gotten far when, a short distance ahead of us, I saw an old, beat-up car. Running up to it not, not even realizing that it might be locked, I discovered one of the doors was slightly open. *We're safe*, I kept thinking. *We're going to live, we're going to live.*

"Carla, its Kris. Hurry!"

I grabbed her, pushing her into the car, and getting into the driver's seat myself. "Oh, no, we have no keys, Lana, no keys." Deflated, I felt tears come to my eyes just as Kris reached the car. Mocking laughter rose in his throat, hatred in his face. Lana had locked the doors, but we both knew it wouldn't be long before he got in. I was about ready to give up when Lana jangled something in front of my face. The keys had been tucked in the visor.

"Go, go, go, Carla, hurry up. Please hurry."

We heard a loud crash and, without even looking, I knew it was Kris. He had smashed the back window and was trying to get in. Lana took something out of her pocket just as I started the car. With a quick glance, I saw she was furiously slashing at him with something. Thank God for Lana.

As I drove away, I heard him scream. Turning, I saw him on the ground, trying to get up. His shirt was covered in blood, his face full of anger, spit coming out of his mouth.

We drove away that early morning, grateful that we were free, but mourning the friends we'd had to leave behind.

CHAPTER 6

We drove in silence. What was there to say? Nothing. Nothing would ever be the same for us again, but at least we had each other.

We drove until we came to the nearest town. Going straight to the police station, we walked in hand in hand—two young ladies bedraggled and covered in blood. What a sight we must have looked. Seeing the two of us in the state we were in, they instantly could tell that something was wrong. Two police officers took us into a room, where they kindly sat us down at a table whilst they sat opposite us with smiles on their faces.

We didn't feel like smiling, but I knew they were only trying to make us feel a little bit better. Between us, we blurted out everything from the beginning to the end, not leaving out one single thing. By the time we had finished, we were totally exhausted. I think our two police officers were too, even though it had been Lana and me doing all the talking. The older officer looked pretty pale.

"So there you have it," I whispered. "It's all true."

One of the police officers got up and quietly left the room. When he came back, two other gentlemen were with him. One of the men was in his early sixties. He had lovely white hair and a great big smile on his face. Immediately, he made me feel at ease. Lana seemed to relax as well.

The other man was in his early thirties, maybe forty. He was taller and very nice to look at with almost black hair. Unlike the older man, he made me feel very nervous. I had no idea why. One of the police officers introduced the two men to us as Detectives Wright and Jackson, the older detective being Wright, the younger man was Jackson.

I suddenly felt my hand being squeezed. It was Lana. Oh, poor Lana, she looked totally exhausted just the way I felt.

"Carla, please can we go now? I want to go home. We can talk later by phone if needed, can't we?"

"Detectives, please, can we go? We are both tired out. We need to get home. Lana and I just can't take any more. We will talk to you later if you want, but not now."

"We understand, ladies, but we need a bit more information, then we'll drive you home, won't we, Fred?" the younger detective said in a grumpy voice. "Hey, Fred, are you listening to me?"

"Yes, I'm listening all right, but I'm afraid I totally agree with these two young ladies. Look at them. They're exhausted and need to get home. We can talk some other time."

I gave him a quick smile, letting him know how grateful I was to him for agreeing with Lana and me.

We all walked slowly to their car. Lana and I sat in the back, totally drained and feeling very, very fragile.

"Oh, ladies, I just needed to tell you that police officers and detectives are on their way to the house right this minute," Detective Wright said. "Just thought you would like to know."

"Detective Wright and I would have gone along, but we were needed here."

It was silent the rest of the way home, which I was truly grateful for. Just very occasionally, throughout the drive home, I heard Detective Jackson burst out laughing at something that had been said between them.

Finally, we arrived at Lana's. I could that tell she was happy to be home. Smiling, she told me to phone her in the next couple of days. Then, giving me a hug, she quickly rushed inside her house, just as Detective Jackson shouted for her to not leave town.

We drove to mine. Seeing my home, I almost burst

into tears, every single emotion wanting to get out. Well, it would have to wait until I was alone. Alone—that nasty little word. Apart from Lana, I *was* alone. It was just Lana and me now.

"Do you mind if we come in?" Detective Jackson asked.

I did mind, very much so, but thought it would be better to talk then rather than later. "Yes, that's fine." Going into the kitchen, I made them some coffee, while I had juice.

"Look, Carla, hey, wake up, sleepyhead."

"Sorry, Detective Jackson," I mumbled.

"Please call me Will." He laughed. "And call him Fred, okay with you, Fred?"

"Sure is, call me whatever you want."

"Thank you, both of you. I am very grateful."

"Please tell us one thing, Carla, how did you know Kris?"

"I once dated him for a short period, nothing serious, though. He went to the same senior school as me," I told them, shifting in my seat.

"Is this Kris?" Fred asked me, showing me a photo.

Even though it was blurred, I knew it was Kris. "Yes, that's Kris."

"Carla, that guy in the picture isn't who you think he is. Isn't that right, Fred?"

"Afraid so."

I choked back tears as they began to fall. "Then who is he?"

"We don't have to talk now, Carla," Will said. "Fred, let's go."

"No, tell me, please."

They looked at me with sympathy in their eyes. I knew they didn't want to hurt me but things had to be said.

Fred patted my shoulder. "That's Seth Armstrong's son Jake. Seth was—"

"I know who he was." I butted in and told them all I had heard.

"Well, that's not quite right," Will said. "Seth Armstrong was never the killer. He never killed anyone, as far as we know. It was his son, Jake, who killed them all. Seth was questioned by police but there was never evidence against him, and Jake…well, he just vanished."

"Where's Jake Armstrong now?"

"We don't know. He's not in prison, we are certain of that."

Fred smiled at me. "The police have been searching for him for a long time with no leads, until now. We only very recently found out that he has been in and out of mental institutions all of his life. He was evil from the time he was born. He never went to school, at least not for long periods. Some of our men have been on the case from day one but, until now, haven't had a single clue where he was. He knows how to stay hidden from the police, so if he's not found now, he may never be."

"Then who was the guy I knew, Officers?"

"What do you mean, Carla?"

"The guy I knew went to school. He was a fun-loving, happy person." I looked from one man to the other. "What are you not telling me?" I could tell, just by the looks on their faces, they were leaving something out.

"Jake had a twin. His name was—"

But before he could finish talking, I almost shouted out Kris. I suddenly understood everything, and the realization made me feel sick to my stomach. It wasn't Kris who had come back into our lives, but his brother Jake.

"What happened to Kris?" I asked, dreading the answer.

"As far as we know, Jake must have killed him at some point and taken over his identity."

I could tell by the pained look in Fred's eyes that he was finding it hard telling me all this.

He took my hand. "Crazy people do awful things and killing your friends was one awful—terrible—thing he did, but it could have been anybody. He just happened to be with you and your friends."

"Maybe—or maybe he wanted to be Kris as he was envious of his life. He's killing everyone Kris knew and cared for. Only someone so evil would do that. He must have hated Kris and—"

Before I could even finish what I was saying, Fred interrupted me. I knew he was doing it for my sake. "We may never know the real reason, Carla, so try not to think about it too much."

"Thank you, Fred I'm grateful for your honesty."

They both looked at me. Were those tears in Will's eyes, or was I just imagining it? They said their good-byes, and I showed them out. Standing at the door, I waited till they got into their car.

Suddenly, not even thinking about what I was doing, I rushed up to the car as they were just about to drive away. Surprise showed on both of their faces.

"His crazy sister, where is she?" I asked.

Fred frowned. "We have no idea who, or where, she is, but she's not his sister, is she, Will?"

"No. Don't you worry about anything, Carla. Call us if you need anything, morning or night."

Not worry? Of course, I would worry. I was scared to death, scared that I was next on his list.

As they drove off, I felt totally defeated. Tears streamed down my face.

CHAPTER 7

I walked slowly into my house, determined to make a fresh start. Lana and I would do it together. Going into the sitting room, I phoned her. There was no answer, so I tried once more. Still nothing, so I left a message on her machine then went to bed. I think I must have slept forever. When I woke up, it was around eleven o'clock the next day, and I was feeling pretty grotty. After having a long relaxing bath, I decided to call in sick. No way was I going to go to work so soon after all that had happened.

My boss was very good, never asked me any questions, which I was very grateful for. After I had something light to eat, I once again called Lana. Still no answer. I was starting to get a bit anxious, but after everything that had happened, she could have been resting. Still, Lana was never one to not answer her phone if she heard it ringing. Something inside of me was bugging me, telling me that something wasn't right. Grabbing my bag, I was just about to leave when the phone rang.

"Lana, about time."

"It's Detective Wright, Carla."

"Sorry, Detective, I thought you were Lana."

He laughed. "Stop calling me detective and call me Fred.

"Fine," I agreed. "Is everything okay, Fred?"

There was a long pause on the other end of the line which made me feel a slight bit nervous inside. I couldn't breathe.

"Can we come by your house, Carla?" Fred asked me quietly. "We'll be at yours later today if that's okay with you."

"See you both later," I said then hung up the phone.

I still decided to go to Lana's, knowing I had plenty of time before they arrived. Picking up my bag and shutting the front door, I made my way to the car, thinking all the time that something was wrong. Trying to block out the horrible feelings, I drove to Lana's. When I arrived, it all looked terribly dark inside. Ringing the bell, I waited, but nothing.

I tried again. Still nothing. I shouted and still nothing. Not knowing what else to do, I left after putting a note through her letter box, telling her to ring me. Then I went straight home to wait for the detectives.

When I got home, I made myself a sandwich and a glass of cold milk then sat in the lounge to watch some television until they arrived. As I sat there, I found it hard to concentrate. My mind was in a whirl. I couldn't stop thinking about my friends. A tear slipped past my defenses, and then I was crying as if I had the weight of the whole world on my shoulders. I cried and cried until there were no tears left. I felt drained but relieved that I had finally let it all out. Shutting my eyes, I sat there quietly waiting for Detectives Wright and Jackson.

It was the knock on my door that woke me. My watch told me it was four o'clock. Letting them in, I took them straight into the lounge. "Please sit. Would either of you like a drink?" I whispered, not really knowing why.

"Carla, sit down, please. We are okay right now," Will said, a half-smile on his face.

Up until now, I hadn't really noticed how handsome he was. With everything that had happened, men were the last thing on my mind. Right then, though, I couldn't help but see Will as a man and not just a detective. Thinking about it made me blush. I felt my cheeks burning. I so prayed they wouldn't notice. Sitting down, I gave them a quick smile, trying not to look at Will, just in case he noticed me blushing.

"Did you get Jake and his sister or whoever she is?

Did you find them, did you find—" I stopped, not being able to say their names.

Will stood. "I'm sorry. No. The house was searched from top to bottom, twice over, but we came up with nothing."

"Not even—" I whispered. "Did you—"

"Stop, Carla, you don't need to say anything else," Fred interrupted and, taking my hand, told me that my friends had been found, plus another five victims.

Tears started running down my face but I stayed calm and strong.

"We are so sorry for all you've been through, Carla. Don't worry, we have all the best people on the case. If they are anywhere to be found, they will be. We promise you that," Fred told me quietly.

Looking at them both, I felt relieved. But still there were little niggles at the back of my mind, telling me something still wasn't quite right.

Will patted my shoulder. "They're long gone. You won't ever see them again. Now you can start getting back to normal, can't she, Fred?"

"She sure can." Fred walked over to the window. "How is Lana?"

"I'm worried about her, especially after going to her place and no one answered the door."

"We'll check on her on our way home," Will said.

"Thank you," I said, showing them to the door. Suddenly out of the blue I shouted, "Stop."

They turned as I reached them, appearing a little worried about me. Their looks of concern were increasing, especially since I nearly fell into Will as I reached him.

"I'm going with you," I told them and quickly got into the car before they had chance to leave without me.

We arrived at Lana's and, from what I could see from the car, it was still in darkness, no lights were on, nothing. I walked slowly behind Will and Fred. My heart was pounding so hard, I honestly thought it would burst. I wanted to be sick, but held it in for all I was worth.

The only thing I could think of right then was seeing my friend again. I knocked on the door. Nothing. I tried again but still no answer. As I was about to shout, I heard a crash.

Turning to the detectives, I realized Will had smashed a window and was climbing in.

He let us inside. "Stay close to us," he told me.

It was very dark and very cold inside. All the curtains were closed, so unlike Lana. She loved the light and kept the windows open. If I was nervous a short while back, I was even more nervous now, not knowing what to think. We went into her kitchen, turning on the lights, then we went into the sitting room. While I turned on the lights, the detectives went to look in the other rooms. I decided to go after them a few minutes later. As I reached the bedroom, Will turned. "Go and wait in the sitting room," he shouted.

I knew something was terribly wrong and fear came over me. I inched my way forward just as Will rushed over to me to stop me. It was too late. There on the bed, with her arms and legs stretched out, lay Lana. She was tied, with some sort of chain, to the bed posts. Blood was everywhere. Her breasts were slashed, almost severed. Her face had bite marks all over it, but worst of all as I looked at her stomach I realized it had been sliced open. I couldn't take any more. I ran out of the room and, right there in the hallway, started gagging then threw up all over the floor.

Will came over to me, making sure I was okay. In the background, I could hear Fred speaking to someone on the phone. I gathered it must have been the police. I was helped into the sitting room where I was eventually given a cup of tea and a biscuit, not that I wanted anything. I didn't, all I wanted was for my nightmare to end, and then I would wake up, finding it all had been one big dream.

I knew that would never happen. My friends were gone forever. I was now truly alone.

The police arrived. Will and Fred left me to go and talk with them and show them around, so I sat silently waiting for them to all finish. By the time they had done everything needed, they had no idea how Jake had gotten in. Someone had thought Jake had used Lana's key.

I let them know that was impossible. "She would never have given keys to him, never."

Fred looked at me. "Then he must have picked the locks."

I honestly didn't know what to think. One thing I did know was that that creep had gotten in and killed my best friend, killed my other friends, and destroyed my life.

"I'm going to kill you, you son of a bitch," I whispered to myself, feeling the anger inside of me.

Fred and Will drove me home, telling me that I could no longer stay there as it wasn't safe anymore. Tears began to fall, this time for the death of my best friend, knowing I would never see her again. Finally, I stopped crying.

Fred took my hand. "Everything will be okay. Different but okay."

God bless Fred. he was only trying to make me feel better. But deep down, I knew I would never be the same again. It wasn't safe with Jake and the bitch still alive, but I didn't want to leave my home and move to the unknown.

Upon reaching my house, Will made a call to someone and then told me he would stay the night, as plans were being made for me to move.

"Until what?" I snapped with anger raging inside of me.

"Until it's all over, Carla," Will mumbled, "and it will be. That's a promise."

Fred said his goodbyes then left, telling me he would see me very soon. Bless him. He had a huge smile on his face, obviously trying to stay positive for me, but there was no way I could be positive. I couldn't even smile.

I gave Will a duvet and pillow. Saying goodnight to him, I went to bed. The next day after we had some breakfast—which I didn't really want, but Will insisted I had to keep up my strength—he made some phone calls. By the time he had finished, Fred turned up. Going into the kitchen, they told me to go and pack. I just stood there, so much anger inside of me. I wanted to let it all out. But it wasn't their fault what was happening to me. It wasn't their fault I had to leave.

I figured they could tell what was on my mind because Fred came over and, sitting me down, he sat next to me. "You have to go into the witness protection program until it's all over."

All over? Would it ever be all over? I prayed to God it would.

Without saying another word, I went and packed.

CHAPTER 8

As we left that day, our spirits, especially mine, were low. There was a sombreness in the air which stifled me. We drove along in complete silence. I knew that if I started to talk all the anger inside of me might come out, and this wasn't the time or place for that to happen.

Maybe Fred spoke to Will. I honestly didn't know. It was all a blur that day. Finally, after driving for hours, we came to a town called Salisbury, which was near the border of Wales. After driving another half hour, we came to a pretty little village called Haven. Just outside of it, I saw a lovely little cottage right by a lake, somehow knowing this was my destination. I was right. It was. If it hadn't been for the whole situation, I would have been completely happy. It was such a beautiful setting and the cottage was right out of a fairy tale. It was pretty and quaint, with a white picket fence—something I had always wanted. We were all grateful to have arrived, to finally be able to stretch our legs. Everyone helped to unpack the car and then, with Will's help, I took all my things upstairs to one of the bedrooms where I unpacked, putting everything neatly away.

Suddenly, I felt so terribly alone. Even though Fred and Will were with me, I knew they would leave at some point. I sat quietly on the bed, scared that if I moved, something bad would happen. Finally getting some strength inside of me, I went downstairs and made my way to the kitchen where Fred had made us all salad and jacket potatoes, which was very welcoming. I must have been a lot hungrier than I thought.

We sat and chatted over supper. They did most of the talking. I was mainly listening to what was being said, even though I couldn't remember most of it the next day. My thoughts were else where.

Fred looked from Will to me. "We'll stay the week to help sort everything out with you. then you'll be on your own."

I swallowed hard.

Will squeezed my hand. "Don't worry, Carla, it will be okay. You can phone us anytime day or night. It won't be forever."

"Thanks for that, Will, thank you both for all your help." I meant it, too. I was really grateful for all their help. I didn't want them to leave.

The week went by far too quickly, almost in one great big blur. I was so glad they had stayed. So glad that I hadn't been by myself. It was going to be hard saying my goodbyes to them now, but had to be done.

During the week, they had been on the phone almost every day, letting me know during one conversation that the police were going to watch my place for a few weeks. If there was any trouble or I needed anything, I just had to let them know. A blue mini was dropped off for me and, upon giving me the keys, they both had smiles on their faces.

I was thankful for the car. It would give me the freedom I needed. It was finally time for them to leave. I was so scared, knowing I was now on my own, truly on my own—finally alone.

Fred hugged me. "Don't go worrying yourself now, Carla, don't ever lose hope. They will be found, we promise you that. Will and I will never stop looking for them, never."

Will hugged me too. "Bye, Carla, good luck."

As I waved them off, something inside of me said that I would never see them again. I prayed I was wrong.

CHAPTER 9

A few months went by. I had finally found work at the library in town, where I worked from Monday to Friday—half days on Friday, which I liked. It suited me perfectly. I loved my job, loved my little home. It had taken me a while to settle, but now I felt at home.

The past was the past, even though I knew I would never forget what had happened. Occasionally, Fred phoned me to have a chat, making sure everything was good with me. We always had a laugh. I loved receiving calls from him. He was the one true friend, the only friend I had left. The police would drive by occasionally, making sure all was good, never stopping for too long, but that was fine with me. It was the reassurance that everything was fine that I needed, and that's what I got from them. As happy as I was, I wasn't stupid. I knew I would never be totally safe, not while Jake and that girl were free. I decided that it I wasn't going to be a "poor me." That was for the weak, and I wasn't that.

I occasionally went out with my colleagues from work, usually just for a drink, the odd occasional dinner. Nothing was said about my situation. No one knew anything about me, which was the way it had to be. I was told to never tell anyone about my past. That was fine with me.

It was a Friday evening when I decided to give Will a ring to see what was happening on his end, if anything had changed for the better. I smiled because part of me just wanted to hear his voice. It was one big excuse to talk to him, but that was okay.

"Well, here we go," I whispered to myself. "Please be in, Will." The phone was ringing on the other end, but there was no answer. It kept ringing, and I decided to hang up. I'd try later—if I dared.

All of the sudden, he picked up. "Don't hang up, who am I speaking to?"

I laughed. "Me, Carla."

"Sorry for taking so long to answer. I was having a shower."

"That's okay, Will. Just thought I would phone in and see what's up. Anything changed for the better?"

"Sorry but—"

"That's okay. Don't worry about it. It's not your fault."

We chatted for a good hour. Nothing special was said, but it was just so good to hear his voice. I felt goose bumpy all over from talking to him, which made me smile. If just talking to him on the phone did that to me, what would I be like if we were face to face? I started blushing.

I was just about to say goodbye when Will surprised me. "Is is okay if I come to visit you?"

I sat there, not knowing what to say. For goodness sake, I hardly knew the guy.

"Carla, is it okay?"

"Sure. I look forward to seeing you, Will. It will be great to catch up."

"I can stay—"

"No you can't," I interrupted. "You can stay with me, Will, sleep in the guest room."

"Great, Carla, see you around eleven tomorrow." He hung up, leaving me in a daze.

The next day came around too quickly. I was excited and nervous at the same time. I liked Will—a lot—but I didn't really know him like I should have. Just because he was a detective didn't mean I should trust him like I was doing.

I checked over the house, making sure everything

was good and that the guest room looked nice and tidy for him. I was probably being a little too fussy about everything, but that was better than being the other way. So I checked everywhere one more time.

Suddenly the doorbell rang, making me jump. It was eleven already. Will was right on time. I started to feel even more nervous, my stomach doing little somersaults as I opened the door. Standing there, I felt my mouth drop open. I had completely forgotten how gorgeous he was, especially now that he was close up.

Will smiled at me, making me feel like a school kid going on her first date. My face felt hot. I had to be blushing scarlet.

Will gave me a quick peck on the cheek. "You look lovely."

It made me blush even more.

After showing him to the guest room, I went downstairs and made us a sandwich and a drink. He finally came downstairs and into the kitchen. I thought he would automatically sit and eat his food. I nearly died and went to heaven when I felt him touch me. Before I had time to do anything, I was being kissed, full on the lips, so tender and so full of passion that I went all hot inside.

"Whoa! Will, I never expected that," I whispered.

"Me neither. You didn't mind, did you?"

I blushed from head to toe. "No, I didn't. It was nice."

He laughed. "Just nice, is that all?"

"W—Will, I'm glad you c—came. I—" I stammered.

"Shush, so am I."

It wasn't just nice, it was lovely, though I wasn't going to tell him that. We sat on the couch together, chatting nine to the dozen. I really had no idea what was said between us half the time, as my mind was elsewhere. It felt so natural being with Will, my doubts fled. I wanted it to last forever. I wanted him like I had never wanted anyone before. I prayed he felt the same.

Get a grip, girl, I told myself *You hardly know him.*

Suddenly, his lips were on mine again, his tongue inside my mouth. I felt like I was falling, my heart pounding in time with his. *Have I died and gone to heaven?*

He was holding me so gently, my eyes glistened with tears. I didn't want him to stop, and I wished it could last forever.

But all good things came to an end in one way or the other. This one certainly did. I suddenly felt myself being gently pushed away from him as he got up.

He kissed me on the forehead. "I'm sorry, Carla. I have a headache, and I'm going to go to bed."

As Will walked out the room, I felt devastated, wondering what I had done wrong. It had been so good between us, and then it was like he hated me. Maybe hate was too strong a word to use, but it certainly felt that way. I prayed that night as I lay in my bed that I had gotten it all wrong and that he *did* have a headache. When I finally got to sleep, I actually slept like a baby. I might have stirred once, but the rest of the night had been perfect.

We both got up around the same time. I felt great…well, maybe a teeny bit nervous, but only because of what had happened. I had some cereal. Will had toast with marmalade and a cup of tea.

"Will…" I needed to say something but I wasn't sure what.

"Don't say anything, Carla. It's totally okay."

"What's okay, Will?

"What happened last night. I honestly didn't mind you coming on so strong. I—"

"Hey, hang on one minute," I snapped, throwing up my hand. "Me come on strong? You kissed me first, not me kiss you, remember?"

"I think you might be right, but whatever. It certainly was good, don't you think, Carla girl?"

It certainly was but I didn't tell him that. The way he was talking to me made me feel a little uneasy but then, with the biggest smile on his face, he pulled me off my chair and right into his lap.

"Happy, Carla?" he whispered in my ear.

Oh, yes, I was truly happy, the happiest I had been for the longest time. Tears came to my eyes, and all that had happened between us last night I put down to him being tired. Forgiving him, I decided not to think about it again or mention it to him.

We walked slowly, hand in hand, into the sitting room.

Will looked deeply into my eyes. "I love you, Carla."

I smiled at him but didn't answer. I didn't know why. No, I did know why. I hardly knew him. Everything was happening too fast, much too fast. I wanted him, I knew that, but not like this. I guess I was old fashioned and, deep down, wanted to take things slowly. Maybe my heart was telling me to be careful. Sitting in silence, I felt all strange inside.

I could tell something wasn't right, but I had no idea what was wrong, and that scared me. I so wanted things to be good between us, and I was scared they weren't. One minute he was all over me, and I really felt he did love me. Maybe love was too strong a word. Then he changed into someone I didn't know. It reminded me of the situation with Jake, and I was frightened that Will would end up being like him. But we had only been together a *very* short time, so I was certainly going to give us a chance.

"Will, are you okay?" I asked when he looked at me strangely.

"Yes, I'm so sorry if I upset you. Please forgive me, sweetheart."

"I know there's something going on—"

Before I could finish, Will cut me off by putting his lips on mine. It was the perfect kiss, making me go all funny inside. As he slowly and gently pulled away from me, I could tell, just by the look on his face, the desire he had for me. I wanted it to last forever, but nothing lasts that long. Still, in the meantime, we could have some fun.

The morning was spent talking, a lot, with an awful lot of kissing going on. That was the best part of my morning, and I was sure it was Will's too. About two p.m., we went off into town where I showed him all the sights. By the time we had eaten something and returned home, it was around six p.m. I was totally exhausted but very happy.

As I looked at Will, I knew without a shadow of a doubt I was falling for him—hook, line, and sinker. He had some funny ways, but I also knew he was kind, thoughtful, and he made me laugh, which I hadn't done for a long time. It felt natural being with him. It made me feel human and, most of all, happy, so that had to be a good thing.

After having a shower—Will ended up in the shower with me—we went downstairs to watch some television, although my mind certainly wasn't on the telly that night. Looking at Will, I could tell he felt the same as me. Later, when we ended up in bed together, his love making was beautiful. I was so nervous at first. Will could obviously tell, so he was extra gentle and loving to me, making me blush from the inside out. Taking things slowly went straight out of my mind.

Tears of pure joy fell down my cheeks. He touched me in places I had never been touched before. It was total ecstasy, and I found myself smiling with sheer pleasure. Laying in Will's arms that night, I knew that I wanted to be with him for always, and I prayed that he felt the same.

As I looked at him, my heart started beating so fast, I feared it would jump from my chest. Could a gorgeous guy like him really want somebody like me? It didn't seem possible. Then he turned and kissed me once more, igniting a fever of desire.

My doubts burned to ashes in the flames that consumed us.

✑✑✑

We got up late the next day. It had been a night of love making and just plain getting to know each other. As I sat eating my cereal, he suddenly blurted out that he wanted to stay.

"Will, did you say what I thought you said?" I asked, hoping I had heard him right. I was so scared I had misheard him. "Will?"

"Yes, my sweet, you heard me right. May I stay, my love?"

"Oh, Will, please stay forever and ever...well, as long as you want, but what about your job, darling? What about—"

"It's all sorted, Carla love. I'm taking an indefinite leave. So we'll see what happens."

I was over the moon with happiness.

Tears of pure joy fell as he took me in his arms and kissed me. I kissed him back and, as his tongue found mine, I knew we were meant to be together. As he finally moved away from me, I saw tears come to his eyes. He turned from me, then, as he looked at me again, the tears had gone and he had a strange look on his face.

"I love you, my sweet Carla," he whispered so low I could hardly hear.

"I love you back, Will, stay with me forever."

CHAPTER 10

As I hurried to get ready for work, it suddenly dawned on me how normal everything was. It had been roughly three months that we had been together. Three *mostly* wonderful months. Every day I got up, I went to work, came home, and was with Will until the next day started all over again.

Hurray, I was finally like everyone else. Will and I were finally like any other couple. I felt so happy, suddenly realizing that for a good while now I hadn't thought of Jake. No more nasty dreams. All that had happened to me was far behind me, and that was where it's going to stay. Will had only just started working at the police station in town. It was only part time, but that was the way he liked it and it fit in well with me. Will seemed happy and contented, and every night our love making was just as passionate and satisfying as it had always been.

Will was still in touch with Fred, which was great. They were partners, so I was very happy to think that Will wanted to stay in touch with him. I usually heard him laughing at something Fred had said, making me smile. I so looked forward to going to bed each night, as our love making just got better and better. When he was inside of me, I felt like we're one, that he was part of me and I was part of him. He was my love, my soul mate. As each day went by, Will and I got closer and closer to each other. I knew he had his funny ways, but I tried to brush those aside.

Sitting chatting in the kitchen a few weeks later, we were trying to decide what to do at the weekend, both of us wanting to do something completely different for a change. What, we were not sure. Suddenly, it came to me—a long weekend away.

"Will, how about a lovely weekend away?" I hoped he had heard me all right as I pretty much blurted it out. I was so excited.

"Sounds wonderful."

Good, he had heard me. I suddenly felt like a school kid again, doing something they shouldn't.

"Are you sure, Will? Are—"

"Come here, sweet Carla."

The sound of his voice right then was so soft and

sensual it made me melt inside. It was all so very tempting to go to him, but we would have to wait until we got back from work.

When I got home from work that evening, I was welcomed by the loveliest of smiles and a delicious kiss which made me blush. I was just about to go upstairs to change when Will grabbed my hand, pulling me to him.

"Hey, Carla, you don't mind me going out with my friends on Saturday and staying overnight, do you?"

"What about us? I thought we had agreed on the long weekend away." I had been so happy all day, thinking about it, and now he had just gone and ruined it all.

Feeling cold inside and scared, I quickly told myself to stop being a silly fool. *Stop being paranoid.*

"Nope, we didn't plan anything as far as I remember."

"What were we doing this morning then, if it wasn't planning a weekend away? What was it then, may I ask?" I was angry now, wondering why he was doing this to me.

"Well, what's it to be then?"

"Go, if you—

Before I finished speaking, Will mumbled something and walked out of the room. Tears filled my eyes, not because I hadn't seen this coming, but because I had totally trusted him. Now he had gone and thrown that trust right out the window. Or was I being just plain silly. I didn't

want to be one of those women who didn't let their partners do anything without them. I wasn't the possessive
type…or maybe I was.

It wasn't particulary good the next two days. I stayed
out of his way as much as possible, not even mentioning
the weekend. Will, though, seemed to go out of his way,
every time he could, to talk about it, to deliberately come
around me always with a smirky grin on his face as if he
wanted to deliberately hurt me. Was I being silly in thinking this way? Was it just my imagination running wild?
Maybe so, but I didn't care. He had hurt me. I had so
looked forward to the weekend away.

Saturday morning came and, as I slowly made my
way downstairs to go into the kitchen, Will came rushing
over to me. I couldn't believe he had the nerve to come
and say goodbye.

"Carla, look, if you want me to stay, I will. You
know, I am—"

"No, you go. We can always do it another time. You
go." I was glad he was going, I no longer felt angry and
upset like I had. I certainly wasn't going to let him off
that easy, but I felt a bit better.

He left, giving me a quick peck on the cheek, telling
me he loved me. I felt totally deflated but, in one way,
glad he had gone. I had chance to be alone, to reflect on
everything. The last few days had been hard. I realized
there was never a proper relationship to begin with. It had

all been based on sex and nothing much else in between. I knew I wanted more than just having sex with a guy, even though, the sex part was wonderful.

Having no proper relationship, however, was asking for disaster. I just didn't want to admit it. I sat in the kitchen, realizing that I didn't want him living with me any longer. We had grown apart very, very slowly, but it had finally happened. Even our love making, as lovely as it was, wasn't quite the same any longer. All these thoughts rushing through my mind made me think that maybe I was being paranoid.

Maybe it was just me putting these silly thoughts into my head because, deep down, I was scared to have a relationship with someone. I knew I had to make my mind up one way or the other. It was one of the hardest decisions to make because I did still love him. I also didn't want to be alone any longer. I just prayed it was paranoia and me being insecure. We had rushed into this so-called relationship, never giving us a chance to get to know each other properly.

I cleaned the kitchen and changed the bedding then went for a drive to try and clear my head. Sitting in my car listening to my music, I finally came to a decision. I knew what I needed to do. Everything became clear to me, as if a weight had been lifted. Smiling to myself, I returned home. After having some lunch, I went for a nice long walk in the forest and down by the lake. It was truly beautiful, making me realize how lucky I was. Right then, all the past was suddenly forgotten, and I knew I wanted to live right here forever. It was just so wonderfully peaceful. No noise of too many cars driving by from morning till night. I walked slowly home, just taking in all the lovely surroundings, talking to myself about what I was going to do the next few weeks for some fun. "Number one," I told myself, "see my friends at work more."

I knew that as soon as Will got back, I was going to give us a chance. We would get to know each other properly, this time.

Then as I turned the corner in front of my house, all my happiness suddenly evaporated. There, on my doorstep, were two mutilated cats with their insides hanging out. Blood was everywhere. Jake was back and I wished Will was with me. I stepped over them and into the house, where I quickly phoned the police. Luckily, they came quickly. After taking photos, putting the corpses in bags to take away, and questioning me, they left, letting me know they would definitely keep an eye on my place. They weren't so sure that it was Jake, but *I* was a hundred percent sure it was.

I was scared. I felt totally alone. I didn't know who to trust. After a short while of feeling down and sorry for myself, I decided to phone Fred. He would know what to do—that I was certain of. I rang his number, the number he told me to phone him on if ever I needed him. No answer, so I tried the station where he worked. They told me he was on a short break from work but would let him know that I had called when he got back. The officer I was speaking to told me to give Fred a ring on his special number and started to tell me what it was. It was the number I already had.

"That's okay, I already have that number. I tried it but nothing, I'll try it later." I thought I had better tell them what happened so I took a deep breath. "Officer," I started, not knowing what to call the policeman I was talking to.

"Please call me Matt. And hang on a minute."

I waited, wondering what he was up to, then, as I was just about to hang up, someone else came on the phone.

"Carla, is that you?"

I didn't recognize the voice. "Yes, who am I speaking to, please?"

"Forgive me. I'm Fred's new partner, Detective Samuels, but please call me Bob."

I told Bob all that had happened, assuming he had already been given the details, as Fred would have told him everything. "I know it was Jake who put those—"

"I know what your going to say, but I think your wrong. You have no proof, Carla. We will look into it for you, though."

"Thank you, Bob. If it wasn't him, where is he then?

Has he been found and that creepy girl who was with him?" I prayed his answer was going to be yes.

"No, Carla, but—"

I clenched my fists, feeling my nails cutting into my palms. I was angry and frustrated because no one seemed to care, and I was scared—more than anything, I was scared I was going to end up dead like my friends.

"I know it was him. He's found me," I shouted at Bob. "Please tell Fred to phone me as soon as possible, will you?"

"Carla, don't go—"

I hung up, not knowing what else to say to him. I'd rather speak to Fred. He would help me.

That night was the worst night I'd had had for a long time. I didn't sleep all night. I was too scared to go to sleep, thinking if I did, I might never wake up. I must have checked the house at least four times, making sure it was as safe and secure as it possibly could be. Although, if someone really wanted to get into the house, nothing would stop them. They would find a way. Jake was going to get me. When, I had no idea, but, in the meantime, I was going to do everything I could to stay alive.

With everything that had happened, I had completely forgotten that Will was due back. Part of me was relieved that he was. We would be able to start afresh, start all over again. At least, I would be safe with him. A small part of me, knew that, once he got back, nothing would change. He would still be the same Will he was before going away for the weekend.

Trying not to think negative thoughts, trying to stay at least semi positive, I just pottered around, not really doing anything.

It was around three p.m. when the phone rang.

"Carla, it's me, Sandy. How are you?"

Sandy was one of my colleagues from work. We got on pretty well most of the time. She was a quiet girl who, like me, didn't really mix with the others, except once in a while. So why was she phoning me now?

"Hi, you okay?"

"I'm pretty good, thank you. I just thought maybe you would like to go out sometime soon. We could go for a drink or dinner if you'd like."

"That would be lovely. Look, let me give you a ring—no, I'll tell you what. We can talk about it at work, make some arrangements to see each other then. I look forward to going out some time." I honestly did look forward to going somewhere with her. It would be a good way of getting to know her better.

"Can't wait," she said. "I don't go out much, and I get a little lonely sometimes."

I knew how she felt and it wasn't a nice feeling. "See you at work, Sandy, stay positive."

"Thanks, Carla, bye."

Almost as soon as I hung up, the doorbell rang. I

knew who it was straight away. It was Will. After everything that had happened, though, I was very cautious and,
instead of just opening the door, I hesitated. "Who is it?"

Will mumbled something under his breath then starting singing—to my disbelief. "Sweet Carla, sweet love,
you are my honey bun, and I am your love."

I laughed so much as I let him in, tears came to my
eyes.

"Am I forgiven? I have been such a prat."

I nodded and smiled at him. "I forgive you, Will. For
the time being, anyway, and use your own key next
time."

I did forgive him as, right then, I needed him. After
giving me a delicious kiss, he went up to have a shower. I
somehow ended up in the shower with him. It made me
forget all the horrible things that had happened to me. I
wasn't stupid. I did know that our relationship most probably wouldn't last. How could it, after all that had happened between us? But I wanted to give us a go.

We made love that night, once more the two of us
becoming one. Once again, it was sheer bliss. He was
gentle and loving, but so passionate, as if he couldn't get
enough of me. I wanted for him to never stop.

As we lay in each other's arms, I could feel his heart
beating in tune with mine, tears fell—tears of pure joy.
We lay in complete silence, apart from the beating of our
hearts.

It was sometime around two in the morning when I heard a noise from downstairs. I could have sworn it was someone moving around. I listened harder, nothing. I looked at Will, but he was fast asleep. I didn't want to wake him, especially if I was just imagining it. So as I lay there, hardly daring to breathe, I just closed my eyes and listened for anything odd. I must have fallen asleep because when I awoke it was ten a.m. Ten a.m. and Will hadn't woken me up. Now I was late for work. As I was about to scream and jump out of bed, Will came sauntering into the bedroom—stark naked, I might add.

"I phoned your work and told them that you needed time off. I phoned mine and told them the same." He had a great big cheesy grin on his face and was looking at me like butter wouldn't melt in his mouth. "You didn't mind me doing that, did you, sweetheart, did you?"

"How long did you get?"

"Two weeks, kiddo."

Part of me said that he had no right to go behind my back like that. He should have asked me first. Something deep down inside of me told me he loved me and wanted to make up for the past, for everything that had happened between us. Now he just wanted us to spend time together. I saw the love in his eyes and I knew, or thought I knew, he loved me. I was going to give him another chance, us a chance. I didn't dare say anything. If I did, it would spoil everything.

I so wanted things to work out between us, at least for now.

As I sat there in bed next to Will, I asked him about his weekend. I thought he would just clam up and not say anything, but it was like he wanted or needed to talk, because he mentioned every little detail, what he had done, where he had been, the friends he had seen. I was happy that he felt he could talk to me about it rather than clam up and not say anything. After he had finished talking, even though he never asked, I told him what had happened to me, thinking or at least hoping he would be concerned.

To my dismay, he was totally the opposite and laughed at me. "It was probably just some stupid kids messing around. You know what they're like, Carla. We were both kids once, and I know I did some really stupid things."

"Oh, like what? You can tell me." I laughed, knowing he most probably wouldn't let on about his past to me. I was right. He just gave me a quick peck on the cheek.

I sat there, feeling a little humiliated and hurt, but I left it at that. He was most probably right about the kids. I wasn't sure about everything else, though.

If I had said something back to him, it would have just fallen on deaf ears. He wouldn't have listened to me anyway. I knew not to talk about any of that any longer.

No more arguments. I was going to give us a go. We both deserved that.

CHAPTER 11

We spent the next few days just enjoying each other's company. Enjoy, I most certainly did. Most of the time we stayed in—making love, watching films on the television, and pigging out big time until we both felt sick. Twice, we went for a walk. When I mentioned driving up to London, he gave me a weird look.

"I'm happy where I am," he said. "I'm enjoying our you-and-me time, Carla."

I left it at that, worried he would get angry with me. All I wanted was for us to be happy together. I was one very lucky person that he wanted me all to himself. I did love being with Will. He made me feel safe somehow, and that's what I needed at the moment, to feel safe.

Okay, he didn't want to go out, but I put that down to not wanting to share me with anyone else, company-wise. Maybe he too felt we should have a fresh start.

The next few days went by slowly, which I didn't mind, but as much as I wanted to be with him, I was starting to feel a little stifled. Nothing to do with Will, I just needed to get out, and not just out. I wanted to get away from the house for a few days.

Looking at Will, I knew I had to mention it, at least. "Will you go away for a few days with me?" There, I had finally been brave enough to ask.

"Carla sweetie, what did I tell you? No, no, no—"

"It's okay, I get the picture," I interrupted.

"Look, why don't you ask your girlfriend Sandy if she will go up to London for the weekend with you. You could both take in a show, do some girlie shopping and bonding."

I was shocked but happy. It was just what I needed. "Oh, Will." I jumped into his arms, nearly knocking him over. "I love you so. Thank you, thank you so much. You don't mind, do you? If you—"

"Go make the arrangements before I change my mind," he said, cutting me off.

I was so excited I phoned Sandy straight away and, like me, she was over the moon. We decided on a show. Sandy mentioned *Cats*, which she hadn't seen. I totally agreed, letting her know that I would make the arrangements for the show and hotel. After talking for another ten minutes, we said our goodbyes, and I told her I would get back to her.

It took me over half an hour to book a hotel overlooking Hyde Park and to book tickets for the show. I gave Sandy a quick ring to let her know the details and that I would meet her at the station Saturday morning around nine a.m., then I hung up just as Will planted a great big kiss on my cheek. I put my arms around his neck, about to kiss him.

"So you want to show me how much you love me then, how thankful you are," he drawled giving me a lovely smile.

"Yes, sir, I do."

"Come then, my sweet, and show me." His voice was so soft and velvety his eyes were pure lust.

He took my hand and I followed him slowly upstairs, where we made love. It was pure ecstasy. I had goose bumps all over me. We couldn't get enough of each other. When I tried to get up, he pulled me down and started kissing me all over, sending little shivers all over my body. When he tried moving, I pulled him on top of me and held his face between my hands, telling him how much I loved him. Our breathing and heartbeats were in tune with one another. I was on fire when his lips started kissing every single part of my body. I felt like I had died and gone to heaven. It was sheer bliss.

That night in bed, I was so happy. Laying against Will with his arm draped over me, I felt I was the luckiest person alive. I could hear him breathing, his heart beating in unison with mine. I wanted to kiss him again, but I wasn't going to wake him. Not being able to sleep, I just shut my eyes, thinking about all that had happened. I thought of my friends, especially Lana, knowing I would never see them again. I was hurt and angry but, most of all, scared. I wanted my life to be back to normal, I wanted to be able to live without ever having to worry about Jake coming for me. I wanted to just live a normal life. With Will? I wasn't sure, even though I loved him dearly. Tears falling, I whispered to myself, "Lana, I miss you. I want you back."

It was around two a.m. in the morning when I heard something scratching at the bedroom door. At first, I thought it was me hearing things, but listening hard again, half asleep now myself, I heard it again. It definitely was coming from outside the door. Someone was outside the bedroom, I was sure of that. As I turned to wake Will, there was a loud bang, someone, something was being dragged across the floor. I could hear the heavy footsteps and the floor boards creaking after each movement. Then I thought I heard someone whimpering, or something.

As I started to panic, Will woke up, looking pretty groggy. "What's up?"

I pointed to the bedroom door, shaking like a leaf. "There's someone out there, Will."

Getting up, he went over to the door. "Stay put," he whispered.

I definitely wasn't going to move. I was too much of a scaredy cat for that. He opened the door and went out into the hallway, closing the door after him. It seemed like forever that he was gone but, by the time he came back, it had only been five minutes at the most. I stared at him, ready for some terrible news.

Will had a big grin on his face. "There's nothing to be scared about. All's was normal in the house. No one had tried to get in. Everything is where it should be."

I didn't believe him because I knew I had heard the scratchings at the door and someone or something being pulled across the floor. I had heard the noises, I was so sure of that.

"Will, look at the door," I whispered.

"Carla, don't do this. Everything is normal, you must have been dreaming, darling."

I stood my ground, knowing he thought I was being silly. As Will made his way to the door, with me slightly behind him, shaking like a leaf, we heard the doorbell ring. Looking at me with a worried expression on his face, he tossed me my robe and put on his. Then he grabbed my hand, and we slowly walked downstairs, to-tally forgetting to look at the door. I didn't want him to open the front door, scared of what we would see, scared of who it would be, but we had to do something. The bell was ringing so loudly, something had to be done about it.

"Please, Will, don't. Please call the police."

"Don't worry, sweetheart."

"Will, I'm really frightened."

I had always acted the strong and carefree woman. Deep down, I was a very insecure person who had always been sceptical and worried over everything. I still was to some extent.

Opening the door first, Will looked outside. Then I did. No one was there. I felt relieved but there was still something niggling at me. Nothing felt right. I went inside while Will fixed the bell then we both made our way back to bed.

"Oh, by the way, Carla, there's nothing. See? Nothing."

He was looking at the bedroom door, and he was right. There were no scratch marks—nothing. Getting into bed, I thought maybe I had dreamed it all along, one big nasty dream. But, still, there was that something inside of me telling me the danger was close by—closer than ever.

CHAPTER 12

We got up early the next day. I was feeling totally worn out, but I decided, there and then, I would put on my happy face and try to have a good day, make the most of things. Looking at Will, I thought I saw a nasty grin on his face. But as quickly as it came it vanished, replaced by a lovely smile. Sitting, eating our breakfast of toast and scrambled eggs, we talked about me and Sandy, London, and seeing *Cats*. After chatting for a while, I started to cheer up. I was looking forward to the next day.

"London, here I come," I sang to myself.

Will, as usual, wouldn't go out anywhere with me that day, so we spent time just pottering in the garden, and I went for a walk. It was the quickest walk I had ever done. Going out down the country paths, I felt like some-one was watching me, waiting for me, ready to get me—

"Stop it, girl," I told myself. "You're being silly."

I kept looking around, but there was nothing but fields and trees, nothing else, no one else, only me. *What paranoia.*

Will and I spent the evening watching telly and chat-ting while the adverts were on. We both disliked the ad-verts, especially Will. It was around eight p.m. when the phone rang. Will went into the hallway to answer it. Turning the telly down, I tried to hear what he was saying but he was talking quieter than usual, so most of it I didn't hear. I was just being nosey, knowing it was none of my business. He would tell me if he wanted to.

About fifteen minutes later, Will sauntered back into the sitting room. He had a strange look in his eyes, almost as if telling me "Don't say anything."

"Who was on the phone?" I asked in my sweetest voice, not caring if he didn't want to talk about it.

"Oh, sorry, sweetie, it was Fred, wondering how we were, asking after you."

"Is he all right, Will? When I tried to get in touch, I was told he was on a break."

"He was. He needed time out and was sorry he missed you, babe. He's fine, though, and will come down in the next few weeks if it's okay—"

"Of course, it's okay," I butted in. "I'm so happy you spoke to him, Will."

We decided to go to bed, as I had to be up early the next day. That night, I slept like a log. The lack of sleep had gradually crept up on me. There was no lovey-dovey that night, just a quick peck on the cheek, but to tell the truth, that didn't bother me. We were both so tired, anyway.

I got up around seven-thirty the next day to have a shower and some breakfast of cereal and toast. As soon I was ready to leave, I noticed Will still hadn't come down, not even to say goodbye to me. I didn't want to have to go upstairs again, but knew I would have to, as he certainly wasn't going to come down to say his goodbyes. Turning to go upstairs, I decided I wanted a goodbye kiss from him. I moved as slowly as I could to go up the stairs just as Will came running down.

"I'm sorry for not getting up. Over slept."

He was just about to kiss me when the doorbell started to ring. I stood there, unable to move. Will answered the door. Two police officers were standing there. My head started to feel fuzzy. I couldn't breathe, scared at what I was going to hear.

"Please come in, Officers," I heard Will say, then everything else was a blur.

They talked. I was suddenly in my own little world, not hearing what was being said, not wanting to hear what was being said, scared of what I would finally hear.

"Carla? Hey, sweetheart, are you okay?"

"Sorry, wasn't listening."

"It's bad news, babe, so sorry. Sandy—"

"What? What about Sandy? What about—" I was blabbing away, hardly knowing what I was saying, too scared to hear what had happened.

"We're so sorry, miss, but your friend is dead."

"Wha—" Nothing else came out. I felt I was falling, falling into the deepest abyss. I would never be able to get out.

Everything went blurry. Will caught me just in time, as I fell to the floor. When I finally came around, I noticed Will was sitting on the edge of the couch, holding my hand. He had a strange expression on his face, as if he was looking at me but not actually seeing me. His eyes appeared totally empty. It was as if I was staring into a black hole. It scared me. *He* scared me, and I knew, as I looked at him, that I didn't want to be with him anymore. I didn't want to give us a go any longer.

Something inside of me said, *No more. Leave him. He's far too dangerous for you.* Feelings? Intuition? I wasn't sure, but whatever it was, I certainly wasn't going to ignore it. I moved my hand away from his.

This seemed to snap him back from wherever he had been, and he gave me a quick peck on the cheek "The police will come by in a couple of days to talk to you."

Getting up, I went out into the hallway, not even thinking it through, and started to reach for the case I had packed for my weekend with Sandy.

Will came into hallway. "Where do you think you're going? I hope you're not planning on leaving me, my sweet."

The tone of his voice scared me. I hated him when he was being all weird, I hated that side of him. It was like he was a completely different person.

"I'm going away for a while, Will. When I get back, I want you gone—"

"What do you mean gone?" he demanded, cutting me off.

"I don't want to see you anymore. It's not working out." I could tell he was getting angry but I didn't care. All I cared about right then was me. My safety.

"Carla, I love you, my darling."

"I am so sorry, Will, I really am, but things aren't good right now. Everything between us has changed, and people are dying, people who know me. I have to go, I'm sorry."

"Hey, I do love you, girl. You know that, don't you?"

"Take care, Will, good luck with—"

"You will see me again, my sweet," he promised, not giving me time to finish what I was saying.

I picked up my case and bag and, without looking at

him, hurried out of my house, tears streaming down my face, tears for all the hurt all that had happened in the short space of time and for all my friends whom I would never see again. I got into my car and drove away, deciding right there and then, things were going to change. Number one—no more men. Not for a long time. Number two—be a strong, assertive woman. Let no one get the better of me ever again.

CHAPTER 13

As I drove away from the house that day, not knowing where I was going, all sorts of terrible thoughts kept entering my head, most of all was the thought of my own survival. I knew Jake was the one who was involved in everything that had been happening. Not only had he killed all my friends, he had also killed Sandy. Whoever I came in contact with, he would kill. It was a fight for survival now, and I prayed that the police would find him before he found me.

I was uncertain where I would live for the next few days, but that didn't matter. I felt relieved because I was finally away from the house and Will. Part of me still loved him. It was his mood swings that I hated. The way he sometimes acted. When I finally did decide to go home, I wouldn't be going back to find Will there, and that put a smile on my face. First of all, I would give Fred a ring, especially since he might phone me, and I wouldn't be there. Stopping on the side of the road, I dialled Fred's number. Nothing, just total silence so I phoned the station, asking if I could speak to Fred.

"Please hold a minute, miss," someone said to me.

I waited a good few minutes wondering what the heck was going on.

"Hello, this is detective Bob Samuels, who—"

"Bob, it's me, Carla Jenkins, what's up?"

"Carla, where are you right now? Please, can we meet up?"

Sitting there in my car, I began to feel cold all over and shivered, not knowing what to say.

"Carla?"

"I'm here. I'll make my way to you. I will be a few hours. I'll see you when I get there."

"See you later, Carla."

We both hung up.

As I drove off, I put on some music, trying to calm my nerves. I was thinking only the worst, so I tried to put good thoughts into my head. I arrived at the police station around three p.m. Burford was a fairly big town, considering were we were. I was lucky I found it as easily as I did, as I had only been here the once before and, of course, that had been in awful circumstances. I did use my sat nav this time, though. I drove into a parking space at the back of the station and just sat for a few minutes. I took a deep breath, got out of my car, and slowly walked inside.

When I entered, Bob was there waiting for me. I couldn't believe it. Though I had never met him, as soon as I saw him, I knew it was him. He was younger than I had expected, tall with short, dark brown hair and a gorgeous smile.

He wasn't what I'd call handsome but he had a very pleasant-looking face. If I had seen him on the street, I would have definitely looked twice.

"I've been looking out for you, Carla," he whispered. "Come with me."

I followed him out to his car, where we sat in silence. It seemed forever, but it was probably only a short while. Looking at Bob, I just knew something wasn't right, and he must have been able to tell how nervous I felt. He took my hand. There were tears in his eyes. Something was wrong, big time. I suddenly went cold all over, shivery inside, even though it wasn't cold.

"Carla, Fred is dead."

"What do you mean, Bob? Dead, how, how—"

"Someone killed him. They killed him." He took a deep breath. "I went to pick him up and found him dead in his basement. He had been tied up and stabbed, with bite marks all over him."

Straight away, I knew it was Jake. Tears fell. "Bite marks?" I whispered.

Bob nodded. "I think you could be right, after all. I think it might be Jake. I have no idea how he could have found you, no idea."

"Bob, I'm scared. He knows my every move and has killed all the people I care about."

"Where are you going to stay tonight?"

"In a hotel. Then tomorrow, I'm going home, my real home in London, as no one knows I'll be there—only you, and I trust you."

"Look why don't you stay with me, I have a spare room. You can sleep in there. No strings attached, Carla, please let me help you."

"I don't know, Bob, I don't want to impose on you."

"You're not. It would be nice to have some company, I don't get it often. Work keeps me too busy to do much else."

"Thank you. I'd like that." I was very grateful. I was scared and confused and really thankful for whatever help I could get.

I followed Bob in my car and, as I drove along, I realized how terribly alone I truly was. My friends had all gone. Fred, who I had been counting on for safety, was also gone. Nothing could bring any of them back, and the police couldn't find Jake and that so-called sister of his. And to make things even worse, I had found and loved someone dearly, then lost them. I wondered if I would ever see Will again. I wasn't sure I wanted to. I really didn't know what to think. All I wanted was to curl up in bed and stay there forever.

I nearly missed a turning from not concentrating like I should have, but just in time I saw Bob turn into another street. I followed. A few seconds later, we drove up a driveway with pretty flowers on either side and a big weeping willow half way up. We parked outside his house. Bob got out of his car and opened his garage door then drove his car into it. I drove mine in beside it. We went into his house, and he showed me around. It was a fairly big house for one person, with three bedrooms and a bathroom upstairs and a fairly big kitchen downstairs, a large hallway, and a huge sitting room full of cosy furniture. I felt right at home, and somehow I knew everything would be okay.

"Why don't you freshen up while I make us something to eat?" he said.

Just the thought of food made me feel hungry. I nodded at him and thanked him for everything. I was so grateful for all his help and for taking me in. I would have gone home, but I truly didn't want to be alone. Bob showed me where I was going to sleep that night so, after thanking him again, I went into the bathroom and washed up.

As I made my way downstairs, I could smell bacon

and eggs cooking in the kitchen. It was a wonderful smell and reminded me of my childhood. We always had eggs and bacon on a Saturday. My mother had made the most delicious breakfast. When my father made it once, he had nearly burned everything. That was the first and only time he got to cook breakfast.

It was lovely just to be relaxing, chatting about anything that entered our heads and, of course, eating our food. After washing up and tidying the kitchen, Bob and I went for a walk to clear our heads. Somehow, we ended up holding hands as we walked along. The whole situation felt so natural to me. It felt nice, normal. Arriving back home, we spent the rest of the evening watching television and ended up in each other's arms, kissing.

"Bob, do you really want this, I mean—"

"I know what you mean," he said, cutting me off. "I'm sorry, Carla."

"I want to get to know you properly first. Let's take it slowly, if that's okay with you?"

"Whatever you want, darling, whatever you want."

I did want him, but it wouldn't be right. I wasn't going to rush into any mans arms again.

My heart gave a little flutter, though. He had called me darling.

I blushed then. My cheeks felt too warm, which made me blush even more.

The sensible side of me said, *Not until you're finally*

safe. The not-sensible side of me said, *I want him to kiss me again.*

But the sensible side of me won that night.

CHAPTER 14

The next day was Saturday so we didn't hurry to get up. It was lovely just lying in bed and, for a little while, not worrying about anything. Finally, I heard Bob get up and go into the bathroom. I lay quietly, listening to the wind blowing through the trees. I looked toward the window. The branches with beautiful colored leaves were gently swaying from side to side, occasionally gently tapping at the window. I smiled to myself, hoping things were finally going to be okay.

Fifteen minutes later, I got up as slowly as possible and had a quick shower. I dressed in an old blue T-shirt of mine and tracksuit bottoms and then made my way downstairs just as Bob was putting the phone down. His face was serious which made me think, *Bad news.*

"Is everything okay?

"Everything's fine, I rang the station to find out if they knew anything more, but they don't."

Fear swamped me, threatening to drag me under. Would they ever find him or the bitch who was with him?

"Carla, we will find them."

I wasn't sure anymore.

We sat in silence, eating our breakfast, then, while Bob was sorting a few things out—papers, etc.—I went for a short run. I felt good being out in the fresh air. It cleared my head, and I realized that, as much as I liked Bob, staying with him wasn't the answer. I needed to go home to Will.

I wasn't stupid. I knew that things had ended badly, but I was willing to give us another go if Will was. I was going to move back to the house and, hopefully, start afresh, even though I knew that, until Jake was found, I wouldn't be totally safe. But Will would be with me. He would keep me safe if needed. After all, he was a police officer. As I ran along, I thought of Fred and wondered why Jake had wanted to kill him. Tears ran down my face. Stopping to wipe them away, I suddenly felt as cold as ice. Glancing behind me, I noticed someone in the distance, staring at me. I couldn't see the face clearly but I knew he was waiting for me. All I sensed was pure evil. Chills ran up my spine. I knew it was *him*, waiting for the right time to finally—

"Hello, sweetheart. I couldn't live without you."

I turned, staring right at Will. He had a big grin on his face.

"Will, I am so glad to see you. I was going to phone you." I took a deep breath as a dark thought suddenly crossed my mind. "By the way, how did you know where I was?"

"I am a police officer, remember? Don't worry. I phoned around." He hugged me. "I am so sorry about what happened. Will you forgive me, darling?"

I just stood there, not knowing what to say, then I remembered the man and turned to look, but he had gone. Maybe my nerves had gotten the better of me, making me think it had been Jake. I prayed that was all it was. I turned back to Will and returned his smile.

"Will, I moved in with Bob," I blurted out, "but I was going to get in touch with you because I'm going to move back and wanted you to move back in with me." I swallowed. "Will, I do love you." At that moment, I meant everything I said.

"I love you too, Carla, and, by the way, I never did move out."

"Great."

We both started laughing. I felt so happy, but then reality struck. Bob. I had to tell him I was going back home, and that was going to be hard for me because I did like him a lot. Mainly though, I knew how much he liked me, and I was the company he truly missed. I didn't like the fact that I would probably hurt him. I felt sorry for him, but I was so glad we hadn't slept together. It would have been wrong and silly. I knew I didn't feel for him that way. I wanted to just go and forget telling him, but that was too cruel a thing to do. Also my things were at his house. I needed them. Will seemed to guess what I was thinking. Taking my hand, he walked me slowly back to Bob's.

"Do you want me to go in with you Carla?"

"No, thank you. I'll be okay." I had to do this myself. Will being there would have made matters worse.

I went in and was just about to call Bob when he appeared from the sitting room. I could tell that he was upset. Even though I hadn't known Bob for long, I could tell something was wrong.

"Bob, you know, don't you?" I saw tears come to his eyes and felt them come to my own. The last thing I wanted to do was hurt him after he had been so kind. "I—I'm sorry but—"

"Don't, Carla. I know what you're going to say."

"I do like you, Bob, but it's Will I want to be with. I love him. You hardly know me. It's best that it stays that way."

"For whose sake, yours or mine?"

"For yours, of course, for yours."

"I'm always here for you, Carla. If ever you need me, I'll be here."

He turned, picked up his keys, and walked out of the house. Knowing that I had hurt him upset me. I didn't want to hurt anyone, especially someone who had been kind to me. Slowly making my way upstairs to collect my few bits and pieces, I knew I was doing the right thing. I was making the right choice. This was going to be the fresh start Will and I needed.

As I walked out of Bob's house that day and out of his life, I knew there would be no turning back.

I moved back to Haven with Will. It was going to be a fresh start for both of us, a chance to start all over again.

That night, as we walked into the bedroom, I sensed the urgency coming from Will. He looked at me with pure love in his eyes, or maybe it was just lust. Whatever it was, it was wonderful. Slowly he undressed me, running his fingers down my body. I then slowly undressed him and, as his shoes came off, we fell onto the bed together, making love all night long. His fingers lightly moving over my body, gently touching my breasts, sent little shock waves of pure joy through me. It was wonderful, everything I had ever wanted and more. I wanted us to be together always. As we lay with his arm draped over me, I believed this was where I was meant to be—with Will.

Tears of happiness came to my eyes. As I lay silently in his arms, I prayed that it would last.

We spent a few days just getting to know each other again, which was great, especially not having to think about work. Will was like a whole new person, which was wonderful, but, as always, there was a tiny part of me that said, *Be careful, girl, watch out*. I pushed those thoughts away. I didn't want to be right.

Maybe I should have just stopped and listened to that negative part of me, but the positive part kept telling me to stop being silly and, as always, the positive part won.

Going to work again was great, just to get out somewhere different and seeing my colleagues. Nothing was mentioned about Sandy, so I kept quiet about it too, since it was such a sad subject anyway. My first day back at work, everything went better than I expected. As I was about to leave work, one of the women asked if I would like to go to lunch with a few of them the next day. I was very surprised at the invitation but happy that they considered me part of their little gang. The next day was Saturday and, since I hadn't planned anything with Will, I said yes. The young woman's name was Jenny Algove. She was an attractive woman with freckles and red hair. Saying my goodbyes to everyone, I left and drove home. I felt happier than I had for a long while. But would it last this time?

It was a lovely bright evening, making me feel even

happier. As I drove up to the house, I sensed straight away that something was very wrong. I had the strangest feeling come over me. I knew Will wasn't home, so that made things worse. Straight away, Jake came to my mind, but he didn't know I was here, or if he did, how had he found me?

I sat in my car, waiting for something bad to happen, but nothing did. There was just dead silence and nothing untoward came flying out of the house. After everything that had happened to me, it was no wonder I was jumpy. I giggled at myself for being so panicky over nothing and got out of the car. As I opened my front door, I breathed a sigh of relief. As far as I could tell, all was normal. Shrugging off my unease, I went upstairs to change. Suddenly, I noticed an oblong box on my bed.

"Will." I smiled, realizing I had spoken his name out loud.

I figured it must be from Will, so I went over to open it. It was covered in pale blue wrapping paper and had a pretty yellow bow on it. I slowly took the wrapping paper off with a half-smile on my face then opened the box. As if in slow motion, the box slipped out of my hands and crashed onto the floor at the same time a black rose fell out of the box. There was another black rose in the box and what looked like someone's finger. Time stood still for me. I couldn't move. I tried to scream but, like in a horror film, no sound would come out of my mouth. I turned and fled down the stairs, nearly knocking Will over as I reached the bottom.

"Hey, kiddo, what's the hurry?"

I pointed upstairs. "Go look in the bedroom," I told him to, not daring to go up myself. I was scared to death.

It seemed like forever that Will was gone but I knew it had only been a few minutes. He came running down the stairs, a big grin on his face. He took a hold of my hand, and I wanted to hit him. Nothing about the situation was funny.

"Carla, it's just a rubber finger."

I didn't care if it was a pretend one or not. Someone had still gotten in and put the box in my bedroom.

"I know it was Jake. He has finally found me and soon he will—"

"Don't do this to yourself," Will interrupted. "Carla, I won't let anyone hurt you. I promise. I will keep you safe, even if it means we have to move."

No way was I going to move again. There had been too many awful things happening lately. All I wanted now was stability in my life. Peace and happiness. I grimaced, knowing my life would probably never end up like that.

"No way am I moving, Will. I'm not going to be chased out of my home again." Right then, I meant every word of what I said, praying it wasn't the biggest mistake of my life.

CHAPTER 15

Will wanted to call the police, but I wouldn't let him. There was no point. They couldn't do anything. There was no evidence, no proof that it had been Jake. The house hadn't been broken into, so whoever had gotten in had to have had a key. There was a fair bit of bickering that evening, with Will almost begging me to call the police, which I thought was strange. But I decided to keep quiet, as I didn't want to upset the situation any more than necessary.

Finally, Will promised that he would go along with what I wanted, but only for the time being. He went upstairs to get rid of the box and its gruesome items.

Suddenly, I remembered I had made arrangements for lunch the next day with my colleagues, but I decided I wouldn't go. How could I, with all that had happened?

"Carla, wake up sleepy head."

I opened my eyes. Will was right next to me. I hoped he hadn't been next to me long, because if he had, then I was going mad for not noticing him.

"How long—"

"Not long enough, Carla," he said, cutting me off.

I smiled sheepishly. "Will?"

"Yes, my love?" he drawled, almost in a whisper.

"I promised some friends from work that I would go out to lunch with them tomorrow." My voice cracked and I could barely get the words out. I hoped he had heard me all right. I was so nervous, I had almost mumbled it and didn't really want to repeat myself.

"That's great. It will do you the world of good. You go."

"Only if you're sure."

The look on his face told me he was sure. His smile said it all.

ოჯო

The next day came too quickly for me. Yawning, I looked over my shoulder and noticed Will wasn't in bed. It was nearly ten a.m.

"Oh, bummer," I muttered to myself.

We hadn't made love at all last night. It had been just

a quick peck on the cheek, then Will had turned over and fallen asleep.

It had upset me a little at first, making me think there was something wrong with me. But we didn't have to make love every single night, as wonderful as it might have been. Most couples didn't have sex every single night.

Stretching, I finally got up, moving as slowly as I possibly could. I then took a quick shower, the quickest ever for me. Usually, I was in the shower for at least ten minutes, if not longer. I loved having the water running over me, washing all my worries away. I decided on a dark blue dress and sandals, which suited me well, then I went downstairs.

"Hello, Carla, I've had my breakfast, what would you like?"

"Err...um." Nothing came to mind, but I decided on a slice of toast and a glass of juice. "Just toast, please, thank you."

Sitting in silence, I ate my toast, occasionally looking over at Will who was busy reading the paper. By the look of total concentration on his face, I knew that trying to talk to him right then was pointless. After finishing my breakfast in silence, which was a rare thing, I went upstairs to clean my teeth and get my cardigan. Looking at myself once in the mirror, I decided I looked okay and went downstairs to say my goodbyes to Will. I wanted to go into town a little early so I could do some clothes shopping, if I saw anything nice, that was. I loved shopping, loved buying new clothes, which I hadn't done since—

My thoughts went back to a time I had shopped with Lana and tears came to my eyes. Rubbing them away, I said my goodbyes, hoping for a great big hug and kiss but, to my disappointment, all I got was a quick peck on the forehead. Not saying anything, I left, feeling totally deflated and slightly angry. I was more angry at myself than at Will, I should have said something to him for almost ignoring me.

Maybe it was me just making a mountain out of a molehill, or whatever the saying was. As I drove along the country roads to the town of Salisbury, I started to feel a lot happier and decided I was going to have a good time with my friends.

I looked in the shops but, in the end, never brought anything. It was one o'clock when I arrived at Tunny's, a lovely little restaurant on High Street. I had never been there before but I knew a couple of the girls had. I was looking forward to trying something different.

"Hey, Carla."

I turned, nearly bumping into Samantha one of my friends from work. She was early like me.

"Thank you for inviting me out, Samantha." I *was* grateful. It made me feel normal again.

"Call me Sam."

I smiled at her, liking her straight away. "Okay, Sam it is."

Ten minutes went by and the others turned up. "Jenny," I whispered to her. "You look lovely today."

She was wearing a dark blue dress which came in at the waist, and her hair was down. Usually, it was tied back. "Thank you, Carla. You look nice too."

Going into Tunny's, we found a table right at the back, out of everyone else's way. After ordering our food, we sat and chatted.

Jenny sat next to me on my left. On my right was Sam. She had a bubbly personality, short wavy hair, and was tall with long legs. Pretty in an odd sort of way. *And she knows it too.* Kerry, who was totally different from Sam, was short with long black hair and was nice looking—not plain, not beautiful, just a nice friendly face. Georgina—Georgie for short—was tall with mid-length blonde hair and a very attractive face.

Sitting, eating my food of salmon and new potatoes, I noticed Kerry staring at me. I knew something wasn't right by the way she looked at me. "Is everything okay?"

"Sorry, but whose that man over there, who keeps staring at you?"

"Over where, Kerry?"

She pointed to the window. Suddenly I felt as cold as ice.

"Oh, he's gone." She shrugged. "He was there, though, and staring at you."

They all stared at me. I felt the blood drain from my face.

"What did he look like?" Georgie asked before turning to me. "Are you okay, Carla? You don't look too good."

"Tall, dark hair, and—"

"Don't," I said. "I have to go."

It had to be Jake. He had found me, he had somehow found me. I shuddered inside. Death was just around the corner for me and for my friends if I didn't leave them immediately.

"Please tell us what's up, Carla," Jenny whispered.

I didn't want to tell them. They probably wouldn't believe me, anyway, but the looks of concern on all their faces made me decide to take that chance. "Okay."

So letting my shield down, which I had promised myself I would never do, I told them everything, from the beginning to the end, not leaving out a single thing. I even told them about being put in the witness protection program.

Shock came over their faces, or was it more sympathy that I noticed? They listened silently, not saying one word until I finished my last sentence. I could tell they were truly concerned about me. Georgie wanted me to tell them more but there was nothing more to be said.

All I wanted was to get out of there. I couldn't breathe. "I'm sorry, girls, but I have to go. Thank you so much for inviting me. I guess I'll see you all at work."

"I'm seeing you home, Carla. Someone should be with you right now."

It was Jenny who spoke to me, bless her. She was trying to be strong for me. Smiling at them all again, I let them know I would be okay. I left them, feeling alone, knowing that I would never be able to see them again. It was far too dangerous. Jake had killed all my other friends. I didn't want anyone else dying because of me.

"Carla, wait." I turned, staring straight at Jenny. The others had gone. No way did I blame them. They had done the right thing.

"Get away from me," I told Jenny. "Don't ever try and be with me. It's too dangerous for you." I almost broke down but I had to stay strong, mainly for my own sake.

"What did you say?"

"Jenny, just go and never talk to me again," I said, far more harshly than I intended.

A single tear slid down her face. "Carla, please let me help you. I—"

"I'm afraid you can't help me. Not even the police have been able to, after all this time. Sorry, but I don't want you or anyone else to get hurt."

Jenny stood up straight and stamped her foot on the

ground. "Hard luck, Carla, I'm with you all the way."

"Please go home. I will see you at work, then we can make arrangements to meet up sometime, I promise."

She sighed then nodded. "Bye, Carla, we'll talk soon."

I wasn't sure she believed me, but she kept walking and didn't look back, which I was so thankful for. Tears in my eyes, I made my way to my car, knowing I could never see my friends again. It would be far too dangerous for them, and I didn't want them getting hurt or killed. It was now time to move on. Where to, I had no idea.

Driving as slowly as I possibly could without upsetting too many drivers, I made my way home, not really sure what I was going to do. The only thing I knew for certain was that Will had to be told. If it hadn't been for Will, I would have turned around right then, driven away, and not stopped until I knew I was safe. I remembered how he had acted, not even giving me a proper kiss goodbye. I also remembered the way he had been throughout our time together, but I still loved him, even after everything that had happened. I didn't know what it was that drew me to Will, but unless something totally terrible happened between us, I didn't want to be alone and without him.

As I got closer to my house, I felt more and more panicky. "Stop it, you silly thing," I muttered to myself.

In the distance, I noticed a car parked next to Will's.

Stopping suddenly, I nearly flew forward if it had not been for the seat belt I was wearing.

All sorts of things came into my head about who could be visiting Will. Why didn't he tell me he was going to invite someone over? Too many dark thoughts came to mind, but I ended up telling myself it was an old girlfriend of his, laughing to myself at all the silly things I was thinking.

Then the front door opened, and my heart missed a beat. It could have been death himself. I wished it had been. Jake walked out of my house, a smirky grin on his face, laughing and talking with Will. As he got into his car, I thought my heart was going to burst. Just seeing him like that, and especially with Will, made me realize the danger I was in.

Luckily, he drove away in the opposite direction from where I was parked.

I felt sick inside. All along, I had been living with someone who was in touch with Jake. All this time, Will had been letting him know where I was, both of them planning my death. In my eyes, he was just as evil as Jake. Will had been smiling at Jake, which sent shivers down my spine. Now, all those little niggles at the back of my mind, which I had never listened to, made sense. It was no wonder Jake had known where I was all the time. They were in it together. Why did they want me dead, or my friends?

Without even thinking about it, I drove straight to the police station, and as I turned to go into the car park, I nearly crashed into a police car coming out. My mind was all topsy turvy. I couldn't think straight. I was going to die.

"Ma'am, are you all right?"

I heard the voice but it was far away, too far. I wanted it to be closer to help me feel safe.

"Ma'am—"

"Carla," I said, "my name's Carla."

"Is she okay? She doesn't look too good to me."

"I'm okay. I'm all right, just a tiny bit dizzy. I'll be good in a minute."

"Officers, you're needed inside," someone with the sternest of voices shouted. Whoever was calling them didn't sound happy at all.

They're in trouble.

"Carla, will you be all right?"

Suddenly it dawned on me why I was there at the police station, and I grabbed the arm of the officer standing next to my car.

"Please don't leave me, I need your help."

"Carla—"

Butting in before they could say anything else. I told them that I was going with them. I got out my car and following them into the station. It wasn't the biggest of police stations, but it wasn't a small one either. It was definitely big enough for the size of the town it was in. Salisbury was the size of Kent.

"Carla Jenkins, what are you doing here?" Turning, I noticed one of the police officers who had driven by my house when I had first moved there, making sure everything was all right.

Even though they had never actually gone into my house, I recognized his face.

"I'm Officer Peters, please call me Jack, though. Are you okay, Carla? You look pretty upset."

Upset? I could certainly think of a better word to use. "Please can we talk somewhere alone, Jack?"

"Of course, please follow me."

Finally, I felt safe, or maybe it was just being in the security of the police station, where no one could harm me.

"Hey, Peters, mind if I join you?"

"Don't mind him, Carla, my partner in crime Officer Pete Jacobs."

I smiled as I was introduced to Officer Jacobs, and I liked them both straightaway.

We went into a small room, which reminded me of a police cell. There was just enough room for the table and chairs. As small as it was, it didn't feel like a police cell, not that I had ever been in one. The walls had been painted a light blue in color, making the room feel bright.

"Please sit, Carla, make yourself comfy."

"Thank you, Officer Jacobs."

"Call me Pete," he said with a smile in his eyes.

I told them exactly what I had seen, who I had finally seen nearly face to face. I shuddered, grateful it hadn't been face to face, or I would probably be dead. The thought made me go cold all over.

"Carla, are you—"

"Yes, Officer Jacobs. I know, without a shadow of a doubt, it was him." It came out a little more harshly than I intended, but I couldn't believe that he would, in any way, doubt me.

"I do believe you, Carla, and please call me Pete," he reminded me with a sheepish grin.

"Okay," I mumbled.

"Would you like a glass of water or—"

"No, thank you, Jack. I'm okay."

Jack rubbed his chin. "Okay, let's think."

I could tell he was troubled. His face had gone all serious. I felt sorry for him and his partner. Being a police officer couldn't be easy.

Pete finally broke the silence. "We have to get you somewhere safe, Carla, where you won't be found."

"Officers, I don't want to be alone anymore. I'm scared. I admit that, but I am also tired of running. I know someone I can go to if you will please phone him for me."

"Who's that?"

"It's Bob Samuels, Detective Bob Samuels, from the Burford police station. I have his phone number."

Giving them the phone number, I stood and started pacing the room while Jack went into the corridor to phone Bob. As soon as Jack entered the room, I didn't even have to look at his face to know that he wasn't happy.

"I am so sorry, Carla,"

Oh, yes, I knew that part was coming.

"Detective Samuels is missing. The police think it's a kidnapping, but they're not sure."

"It's Jake and probably even Will," I told them. "All my friends are dead because of them, all the people I care about, and now Bob, because it's the only way they can get to me."

"We tend to agree with you, Carla, don't we, Pete?"

"Sure do, sure do."

"Please find Bob. He's—" I felt devastated. He was my friend, like everyone else had been. Now they were all gone. I prayed he was alive.

"The police at Burford are doing all they possibly can. They think either Jake or Will will try to get in touch with you. They will phone your mobile, so keep it with you always, Carla."

I thanked Jack for letting me know what to expect. "But what's going to happen now, where will I go?" I felt like crying but didn't want to do it there, not in front of them both. I had to be strong, for now.

"We could put you into the witness protection program again but, knowing that you don't want that, for now we will put you into a safe house."

"What does that mean, Pete?"

"It's a house where people who are in trouble, like you, are sent—people who are waiting to testify, mainly. It's about an hour's drive from here to Chingford."

"I've never heard of Chingford, but it sounds good enough for now." I paused as a thought occurred to me. "What about my clothes? They're all…well, you know where they are. What am I going to do?"

My clothes were not important, compared to my life, which was very important. I didn't want to die. I wanted and needed to live. I needed to live to watch Jake and Will, and that bitch, be put away forever. The thought of going away again, even if it was to some safe house scared me. I would still be alone.

"No you won't, Carla."

"How did you know what I was thinking, Jack?"

"It was just a good guess."

As I looked at him properly, I realized what a good-looking man he was. He had short, dark brown hair and dark brown eyes. They were friendly eyes, kind eyes. He was around six feet, maybe a tad bit taller, not much, though. He was about forty years old. Pete was the older of the two of them, maybe in his fifties. He was nice looking with blond hair and pale blue eyes. He had a kind face. He wasn't as smiley as Jack, and he was also short-er, around five feet ten. I quickly stopped looking at them and, instead, started pacing up and down—as best as I could in such a small room.

"Carla."

I stopped my pacing and stood, just trying to take everything in. It was hard because my head was spinning. "Sorry, Pete, please carry on."

"You won't be alone at the safe house. A lovely lady called Sylvie Dorson stays there. She's our housekeeper and caretaker there. She takes care of everyone who has needed to go there. You'll like her."

I felt a slight bit better as Pete said that, and especial-ly the bit about me not being alone. That was certainly good news. I had hated the idea of being totally alone. All sorts of thoughts came to my mind, but I didn't say any-thing right then.

CHAPTER 16

That night, as we drove away from Salisbury police station, a feeling of doom came over me, then it vanished and all I felt was numbness. I was so grateful for all they were doing for me, for all their help. I wondered if they were feeling as scared as me. If they were, they certainly didn't show it.

By the time we arrived at Chingford and the safe house, it was dark so I couldn't tell what anything looked like. I almost fell out the car from sheer tiredness, only just stopping myself from reaching the ground. From what I could see of the house, it looked like a normal four- to five-bedroom in a cul de sac. I had no idea what the time was but didn't really care. All I cared about was getting some sleep.

We didn't have chance to knock at the door. It opened before we even reached it. A kindly looking lady stood there with a big smile on her face. The smile was infectious, making me smile back. She had gray hair and beautiful blue eyes. She was the typical grandmother type that everyone would want. I liked her immediately.

Pete shook my hand. "Carla, this is where we leave you, I'm afraid. Jack and I will be back in a few days' time to see you. In the meantime, Sylvie will look after you."

"What about clothes and—"

Sylvie put her arm around me. "Don't worry about all of that, my dear. We will sort everything out tomorrow."

I nodded. "Okay, and thank you so much for everything, Mrs. Dorson."

"Please call me Sylvie, my dear, and we'll get on just fine.

Jack handed me a piece of paper with a phone number on it. "Carla, if you need us at any time, just ring this number. Don't go out of Chingford and you will be okay."

Okay? I would never be okay again. "How do you know they won't find me here? They—"

I couldn't speak. My throat felt like there was a giant lump in it. I felt too emotional and, if I said anything else, I would burst out crying.

Pete patted my shoulder. "Please try not to worry about anything right now, Carla. We will be back in a couple of days. Jack and I will be in touch with Burford police station, and we will keep you posted on everything that's happening, that's a promise."

"Thank you, both of you, for everything." I was very grateful to them—very grateful to the police in general.

As Sylvie and I stood, waving them off that night, the strangest of feelings came over me, as if someone had just walked over my grave.

∽✺∽

The next day, as promised, was spent getting clothes and other bits and pieces that I needed. Buying new clothes was great, when it was done in a normal situation, but of course this was no normal situation, and I was glad when we had finally finished buying all that I needed. Sylvie spent time showing me around Chingford, which was a charming, picturesque town.

There were plenty of shops—all the ones one needed—with lots of pretty lanes, which were mostly full of oldly-worldly building. By the time we got back home, I was worn out but felt a whole lot brighter than the night before.

I knew life, for me, would never be the same again, but I made up my mind that I was going to make the most of it and try to stay positive for everyone else's sake, and especially for the people trying to help me.

I spent the rest of my morning trying on my new clothes, and, by the time, I had finished, several hours had gone. I had taken it slowly, putting them on then looking at myself in the mirror to make sure they looked good. When I was done, I went downstairs and walked into a bright sitting room where there was a big antique bookcase full of different types of books. Reading was always something I loved doing, so I chose one out of the novel section and sat reading. I heard music playing, some beautiful music which I was certain I had heard somewhere before, a long time ago. Getting up, I headed out to go find Sylvie. As I got to the door, Sylvie came into the room, smiling and cheerful.

"Sylvie, what's the music you were just playing? I'm sure I've heard it before. I think my mother used to play it."

Listening to the music had made me think of my mother. Tears came to my eyes as I prayed I would see her again. My father had died when I was young. I didn't want to lose my mother, or worse still, have my mother lose me, as I knew she wouldn't survive well without me around. My mother had never married again, for which there were some regrets there on her part. "Never found the right one, kiddo, no one like your father," she would always tell me.

"Carla, are you okay my dear?"

I smiled, mainly to myself, but also to reassure Sylvie I was fine.

"I was just playing a symphony from Beethoven," she continued. "It's one of my favorite pieces of music."

"Yes, it is beautiful. It reminds me of my mother. She used to play it all the time when I was younger."

"I'm going to make supper soon. Is there anything special you would like, my dear?"

I shook my head. "Whatever you want to makejsut is fine with me."

While Sylvie went off to make the food, I went to freshen up before supper. I took a quick shower before I headed downstairs that evening. I felt a lot better than I had in a long time. Things were not perfect. If they had been, then none of this would have ever happened. But for now, I could live like this. Well, at least I was going to give it a jolly good go. Besides, it was a simple case of living this way or probably being killed. If I had been given a choice, I would rather be at home, my own home before this all happened.

ꘛꘛꘛ

Like they promised, Jack and Pete turned up two days later with a present for me. It was some of my belongings that had been at the house, along with some jewelry that my mother had given me.

"Thought you would like these few things, Carla. Hopefully, they'll make you feel a little more at home."

I smiled at Jack. I was very grateful. The jewelry was very precious to me, so I was thankful for that, most of all.

"Did you see—" I stopped. I couldn't mention their names.

"They weren't there, were they, Jack?"

"No, the house was empty. Looked like they had gone for good. The police will be keeping an eye on the place for a while, just in case they do decide to go back there."

I started to shiver—not from the cold, because it wasn't cold—but from Pete mentioning Jake and Will.

We sat out in the garden. It was a lovely big garden with two apple trees at the bottom and a shed. There were pretty colored flowers all around the edges of the garden, making it look like something out of a fairy tale. All of us sat at a table on the patio with glasses of homemade lemonade.

We sat in complete silence, which gave me time to ponder things.

Sylvie sighed and stood up. "Time for me to get out of your way. I'll see you in a little while. my dear." She winked at me as she left us, making me giggle.

Pete turned to me. "We are sorry, Carla, but right now we can't tell you much."

I knew that was coming. I felt angry inside. It was all taking so long.

"The police and detectives at Burford are doing all they can. It's the waiting game."

"What do you mean, the waiting game, Pete?"

"We just have to wait now, hoping for a telephone call. Pray that one of them will phone you. That's why we said to keep your mobile with you always, day and night. Everyone's doing all they can in the meantime."

"What—what if they don't call, what then? What will happen to Bob?"

My eyes filled with tears. This was all my doing. If I had never met Bob, he would be safe today. I felt guilty as hell and prayed that he was still alive.

"Don't do this to yourself, Carla." Jack held my hand tightly. "Don't blame yourself. This is not your fault. It could have been anyone of us."

Maybe Jack was right, or maybe he was just trying to make me feel better. I was grateful that people cared enough to help me. This case had gone on too long. I prayed it would all be over soon.

Pete looked at Jack then me. I felt a slight bit anxious at what he was going to say. "Please, is there is something your not telling me?"

"There is. We have been talking to different people about your case. Doctors, psychiatrists, a couple of close friends of Jake's family. We may never know the whole truth. We know that he killed your friends and at least thirty other people. Mainly women. He's been in and out of mental institutions since the age of fifteen. His parents couldn't cope with looking after him. His last psychiatrist said he should never have been let out of the hospital. If it had been up to the doctor, Jake would still be there. He is a schizophrenic who hates people, especially women."

"Why women?"

"His mother was beautiful. Her friends said she flirted with all the men. She would do it in front of her children and husband. Something he saw when only very young must have triggered it. One close friend of the family thinks that possibly sex between mother and son went on. From a young age he hated girls—women. In that young, immature mind of his, they were disgusting, nasty people who needed to be taught a lesson."

"Its like children who hate animals, especially cats, so they harm them. Unfortunately Jake hated people, which has turned to murder."

"Why his family though, people who cared for him?"

"It didn't matter that they were family, they were women."

"Some of my friends weren't, though."

"He saw an opportunity, took over his brother's identity. So in a way, to him he had to do what his brother would—was—doing. Getting in with all of you was just one excuse for him to go on a killing spree, not caring who it was. He's playing cat and mouse with you, Carla."

"One thing I need to know. Who is Will to Jake?"

"We don't know—someone he met while in one of the hospitals, maybe, but as I say, we don't really know. The girl, we found out, was in one of the hospitals he was in. Why he hasn't killed her too is beyond us. One of the doctors whom we spoke to thinks he must have seen something in her that he never did in anyone else."

I frowned. "Maybe it was just sex he wanted, so he got it from her. Just kept her around for that only."

"You could be right there Carla."

We talked a little while longer. I was really glad they had come. With them around, I felt safe. I frowned as they finally got up to leave, wondering when they would come again.

Jack took my hand in his, making me feel warm again. "We will be back soon, Carla, so try not to worry about anything."

That certainly was the most ridiculous statement of the year. I pulled a funny face at him, and he laughed. Holding my hand like that, he made me feel like a woman. He made me feel attractive and wanted.

There was something about him that put me at ease, and it felt so right being with him. But I had been fooled before, and I wasn't sure I wanted another relationship.

Pete tugged Jack away. "Goodbye, Carla, stay positive."

"Thanks, Pete, I will certainly try, for you two."

"We will be back soon. Phone us straight away if you hear from them."

Sylvie came out as they turned to leave, and we both stood waving them off.

൦൭൦൭

That night, my nightmares came back. I saw myself running, though from what, I couldn't see. Whatever or whomever was after me scared the living daylights out of me. I could hear wicked laughter behind me, but each time I looked, I couldn't see anything. It was total darkness, but I knew it was there, lurking in the shadows, waiting for the right time when—

"Wake up, Carla, wake up, darling. It's just a dream."

I heard screaming from a distance, which seemed to get closer and closer. I tried to see where it was coming from then realized it was me.

"Hush, hush now, dearie, it's only a dream." Sylvie held me in her arms and, once again, I was safe.

CHAPTER 17

Carla, it's been almost three weeks, and you've only been out three times since—"

"I know, but I'm good and I've had no more nightmares since then, so stop worrying, okay?"

"Maybe we could go out tomorrow, take in a movie. Whatever you would like to do."

Bless her. I knew she meant well, and I was truly grateful for everything. I felt useless, though. I knew I needed to do something, but what?.

"Carla, you can talk to me. I'm a good listener."

Smiling, I took hold of Sylvie's hand, and we went into the garden.

It was a lovely day outside, a day for getting out and enjoying the sunshine. Sylvie put the shade up as we sat at the table, making it just perfect, so we wouldn't burn in the sun.

I started mumbling about needing to work.

"What was that, my dear? I couldn't hear you too well."

"I'm thinking of getting a part time job down at the library if they will have me. What do you think?"

"Good for you. It will do you a world of good. What made you decide this?"

"I'm fed up and feel useless. Doing something will help me a lot, at least take my mind of things, even if just for a little while."

"When are you going to phone them?"

I smiled at Sylvie, happy she agreed with me. "I've decided to go down and talk to them. Will you come with me tomorrow morning?" I could go by myself but, for some reason, I felt I needed someone with me.

"Of course, I'll go with you, my dear. We can make the most of it and have a fun day out."

"Sounds good to me, and thank you for everything, Sylvie."

I spent the rest of my day doing a few chores to help Sylvie and then, after taking a long hot bath, a lot longer than I normally would, I rang Jack. I let it ring a while but there was no answer, so I rang again, leaving a message. I felt excited about getting a job. It wasn't anything special for most people, but for me it meant a little bit of freedom. I would also meet some new people. I had dinner by myself that evening, as Sylvie went to see an old friend of hers whom she hadn't seen for a while. There was quite a lot of "I really don't think I should leave you," and "Will you be okay?" from her until I put my foot down and almost shouted at her to go. We ended up giving each other a hug and, finally, she left.

I watched some television but kept flicking from one channel to the other after a while. I felt fidgety so I turned the television off and tried phoning Jack again.

He answered straight away, making me smile so much I thought my face might crack.

"Carla, it's so good to hear from you. Are you okay?"

Okay? I felt more than okay right then, but didn't tell him that. "I'm great…well, as good as possible, Jack. Just wanted you to know I've decided to get a part time job at the library. What do you think?"

"That's good news. I'm happy for you. I really am. It will do you a world of good."

"Thank you for agreeing with me." I paused, thinking of his marvellous grin, and it made butterflies squirm in my stomach.

"Carla, are you still there."

"I'm here. Is everything okay down there?"

Before he could say anything, I knew what his answer would be—intuition or maybe just a good guess?

"Everyone possible has been searching all the places where we think they could be. We have come up empty handed. It's like they have totally disappeared."

I sighed, not knowing what to say. "What about Bob?" I immediately felt guilty. I hadn't thought of Bob for some time, as Jack filled my thoughts most days.

"We haven't found him yet but I promise you we will, Carla, we will find him."

I was sure that Jack was only saying it for my sake. If they hadn't found him by now, they never would.

"Carla, are you—"

"I'm fine." I didn't really want to talk any longer. I knew the police were doing everything possible, but it still didn't make things easier for me.

We talked for a few more minutes, then Jack said his goodbyes, telling me that Pete and he would be down to see me in a couple of days. Soon after the phone call, Sylvie came in, which pleased me. I somehow felt safer with her around. We talked for a short while and Sylvie told me all about her friend. She sounded like a lovely lady just like Sylvie, all bright and bubbly. It was around eleven-thirty p.m. when we said our goodnights.

Lying in my bed, all I could think about was death. I tried as hard as I could to have good thoughts come into my head, but nothing nice seemed to want to enter, so I tried thinking of Jack and, very, very slowly my mind drifted far away…

❦❦

It was out there again, but getting closer as each minute went by. I turned, but all I could see was total darkness. My heart was beating so fast, I thought I was going to die. I could hear hissing and wailing right behind me. I ran, knowing that somewhere, there in the dark, was waiting for me, ready to grab me. I stumbled, but managed to stay upright. About to turn around, I smelled an evil stench behind me. I tried to move but couldn't. I was falling right into the deepest abyss and couldn't get out. I knew then that death had finally gotten to me.

❦❦

"Carla, shush. You've been dreaming again."

I was covered in sweat and tears and shaking so badly I thought I would never stop. It might have only been a dream, but while it was happening, it had seemed far too real, as if I was actually there and being chased by something evil. I believed that if I hadn't woken when I did, death would have taken me.

"Hush, hush, my dear. It's going to be all right. It was only a dream."

"He got to me, Sylvie. I couldn't get away. I tried so hard to—"

"There, there, my dear. It's going to be all right. No one's going to get you. Go back to sleep."

I'd never be able to sleep for the rest of the night, but I pretended that I would be okay. After she had left me, I lay there, praying I would survive all of this, and no one else would be hurt.

It was around ten a.m. when I finally woke up. I felt pretty grotty after such an awful night. I thought I would never fall asleep. I hadn't wanted to, just in case I never woke up again. But I had finally dropped off, and now I was awake and alive.

After having a shower and dressing in a navy blue sweater and sweat pants, I slowly made my way downstairs. I felt like turning around and going back to bed but carried on. I could smell bacon and eggs. Just the smell made me feel sick, but I walked on into the kitchen.

"Good morning, my dear. How are you feeling?"

"Not too good, but once I get out I should be fine. The fresh air will do me good. I'm looking forward to going out."

"What would you like to eat, Carla?"

"Nothing for me, thank you."

"How about if I make you some scrambled eggs on toast? You must keep up your strength. What do you say?"

"All right, thank you, that sounds lovely." I was glad I said yes. It was very nice and made me feel a whole lot better than when I first got up.

We decided to wait until after lunch and then go into

town, giving us time to clear up. Sylvie also had one or two jobs she needed to do.

I helped wash up the breakfast dishes then went upstairs to freshen up and brush my teeth. I went downstairs, feeling so much better. I felt glad to be alive. Sitting in Sylvie's library, I started reading one of her autobiography books about the US President Obama. I must have dropped off, but only for a short time.

Sylvie stood over me, stroking my arm gently, telling me to wake up. I smiled, letting her know I was okay.

"Lunch time, sweetie."

"Thank you, I'm hungry."

Hungry? I couldn't believe I had said that, but I was. I was actually hungry.

We had salmon and salad, which went down nicely. It was around three p.m. when we arrived at the library. While Sylvie went off to look at the books, I spoke to one of the ladies who worked there. Her name was Mrs. Latimer and, luckily for me, she happened to be the boss. She was very pleasant and very helpful, telling me she would love to have me on their team part time. I was to start on Monday.

I went away with Sylvie that afternoon, feeling very happy. I couldn't stop smiling. We decided to take the long route back. It felt so wonderful just to be out. We had the car windows down so I could keep breathing in the fresh air. Sylvie seemed just as happy as me. She had a great big smile on her lovely face. I touched her hand gently, just to let her know how grateful I was for her. Right then I thanked God I was alive.

As we slowly started to turn into our street, something made me shiver inside, and I sensed something wasn't right. I didn't know why I felt something strange, because there was nothing out of the ordinary to see. The street seemed normal, but I just knew, by the way I felt, that all was not right. I shuddered, making myself jump.

Parking the car outside of the house, Sylvie turned to me, concern on her face. "Carla, what is it?"

"I'm not sure, Sylvie, but nothing feels right, I don't know."

"Shall we call the police?"

"Not yet, but I want you to stay out here." I knew just by the look on her face that she didn't want me going in alone, but I had to. There was no way I was going to put Sylvie in any danger. Too many people had already been killed because of me. I was going to make sure that didn't happen again. I turned giving her a quick hug. "If I am not out within five minutes, call the police, Sylvie."

My blood froze as I walked up to the door, praying I was wrong but somehow knowing I wasn't. As I walked inside, closing the door behind me, I saw straight away I wasn't wrong. The hallway was full of Sylvie's lovely pictures that had been hanging on the walls. They were all smashed to bits. Glass was everywhere.

As I walked into the lounge, I felt tears come to my eyes. All the furniture was broken, the room was a mess. You couldn't walk around in it, for fear of tripping over something.

I stood there, unable to move. Suddenly, I felt a hand touch my shoulder. I screamed, turning around at the same time, ready to lash out at the person behind me, thinking my time was up.

"Carla, it's only me."

I felt so happy to see Sylvie, relieved it was her and not the killer.

"I haven't been upstairs yet," I whispered to her, scared of who might hear us.

We stood there as quiet as two mice, just looking at each other, not daring to move. Something moved on the landing upstairs. Someone was sneaking around up there, ready to pounce. They had finally found me. I grabbed Sylvie's hand and we were out of the house quicker than Superman.

"Call the police, Carla."

I didn't need to be told. As soon as my foot was out of the house, I rang them on my mobile.

We both sat huddled together in the car, praying they wouldn't be long and that Jake and Will would still be in the house, so the police could get them, and I would finally be able to live a normal life again.

I knew it was them. I didn't have to see them face to

face. I had smelled the evil stench coming from them, like I had all those other times.

Two police officers turned up five minutes later, which we were so thankful for.

"Officers, they're in the house. They've found me."

"Sorry, ma'am, but what are you talking about?"

Looking at their surprised faces, I realized they knew nothing about my situation. They must have thought me a right lunatic.

Sylvie bristled. "Please hurry, Officers. There's someone in my house. Don't just stand there."

As they went into the house, a police car drew up and two kindly looking police officers got out, smiling at both of us.

"Do you know the situation, Officers?" Slyvie demanded.

I smiled at her, glad she was taking over. I felt drained.

"Yes, we know all about Miss Jenkins's situation. We are truly sorry for everything you have been through, ma'am."

"Thank you, please call me Carla, Officers."

"Please wait here a moment. Sorry, I'm Officer Mayer, and he's Officer Stone." The officer pointed at his partner, who was talking with the other two officers. They had finally come out of the house.

Both Sylvie and I sat in the car, waiting patiently

while they talked. She looked totally worn out, bless her. I felt so sorry for her.

If it hadn't been for me, she wouldn't be in this situation. I knew I had to keep her safe. I didn't want her to die like all my other friends. I didn't want anyone else killed because of me. Why this was all happening?

"Carla, dearie, are you all right?"

Her face was full of concern, making tears come to my eyes, which I immediately rubbed away. "I'm hanging in there, Sylvie. How about you?"

"Please don't worry about me, sweetie. I'll be fine. It's you they're after, not me."

I frowned. "No, it isn't just me. Everyone who has come in contact with me has been killed. Bob is most likely dead, and if he isn't right now, he will be. They won't let him live. All my friends were tortured, not just killed outright. That would have been bad enough, but they were tortured in the most horrific ways possible."

Tears started to flow as I thought of my friends and the horror they had gone through. We watched as the two police officers who had searched the house drove off. They obviously hadn't found anyone. I knew until they did find them, I would be forever running. "Officers, they didn't find them, did they?"

"They have searched everywhere, Carla, and came to the conclusion that it probably wasn't them in the first place. We tend to agree with them."

Sylvie narrowed her eyes. "Officer Stone, why do you think that? They could have found Carla, couldn't they?"

"Yes, ma'am, but in this instance, we think that's highly unlikely."

I gulped, certain they were wrong.

"We will keep an eye on your home, Mrs. Dorson, but we are pretty sure it's not anything to do with Jake and Will."

"Why do you think that, Officers? Why couldn't it be them?"

"Because, Mrs. Dorson, we know that there have been robberies in this area, and we are pretty sure that's all it was. Would you like us to help you clean up all of your mess?"

"No thank you, we'll manage."

I gave a small sigh of relief as the police officers drove away, even though, deep down, I knew that it was Jake and Will, and maybe even the bitch had been with them. Somehow they had found me. How they had found me was my biggest concern, because I simply had no idea how they could have. Maybe the police were right. Maybe it was just thieves, after all.

Sylvie and I worked really hard, cleaning up the hallway and sitting room, even though we were already exhausted, especially Sylvie. But finally we managed to get it all sorted, knowing that new furniture would have to be bought. Sylvie knew that she would have to get things sorted out with her insurance company to get the money back for new furniture. Luckily, when we went around the rest of the house that evening, all was where it should have been. Thank goodness it had only been the hallway and sitting room which had been ruined.

For the first time ever, she looked totally drained. It was as if she had aged ten years. I took her hand and led her into the library, giving her a glass of sherry. I would have to move on. Staying with her was out of the question, as much as I wanted to. I had grown very fond of her, so having to leave was going to be really hard for me. But if I stayed, something bad would happen to her, and I didn't want someone else dying because of me. Her life was more important than my loneliness. We both went to bed that night, totally drained of energy.

I felt like giving up and letting what was going to happen to me happen, but I knew that was the tired side of me talking. By the morning, I would be thinking positively again without so many negative thoughts. Life could have been worse. I just wasn't totally sure how...

❧❧❧

As I sat up in my bed, the awful stench was all around me. I looked around, but everywhere was pitch black. All I could hear was wailing and gnashing of teeth.

I tried to move but my legs felt heavy, as if something was on top of them, holding me in place. I screamed for help, but no one came. I knew I was in hell with no way of escaping. It was the total darkness that terrified me—not being able to see anything. I tried to move again but still my legs wouldn't budge, so I reached down to feel them. There was nothing there where my legs should have been. I started to scream, knowing I would never stop.

ↄↄↄ

"Carla, Carla sweetheart, wake up. It's just another dream."

"I thought they had gone, Sylvie. Nothing was there, nothing—"

"What wasn't there, Carla?"

As I looked at Sylvie, I realized I was safe—once again, it had just been an awful dream. "It was so vivid this time. I thought they weren't there." I reached down to touch my legs. Tears came to my eyes, but I quickly rubbed them away. "My legs. I had no legs." I stopped, not daring to say anything more, just in case it actually happened. They said dreams couldn't become reality, but I wasn't sure.

I couldn't sleep the rest of the night. I didn't dare, just in case I had another terrible dream and this time never got out of it. I must have, at some point, dropped off, because when I finally opened my eyes, it was past eleven a.m. I took my time getting up, as my whole body felt totally wrecked, as if a train had driven over it.

I had a quick shower, washing my hair at the same time, then dressed in blue trousers and a cream-colored top. Checking myself in the mirror, I thought that, for someone who had gone to hell and back, I looked pretty good.

When I reached the bottom step, I called Sylvie, just to let her know I was up, but there was no answer. I went into the kitchen, thinking she might be there making some breakfast, but it was totally empty. I looked everywhere else, but the house, apart from me, was totally empty. I stood in the sitting room, paralyzed with fear, praying Sylvie was all right.

If she had gone out, she would have left a note, but there was no note to be found. I didn't want to start panicking. After all, it could have been a mistake on her part and she forgot to leave a note. With all that had been going on, I knew if my head wasn't attached to my body, I would lose it. I decided to have some breakfast so I headed for the kitchen. I felt odd sitting by myself eating my breakfast as I generally had it with Sylvie.

I decided not to go into work, even though I knew I might be sacked straight away when I did go in the next day. After everything that had happened, I would be no good to anyone that day, I felt like a total wreck. I rang and asked to speak to my boss, who was very nice and, luckily, didn't ask too many questions. I pottered around then went upstairs to freshen up. Just about to clean my teeth the phone rang, I prayed it was Sylvie.

"Sylvie, thank goodness you—"

"Miss Jenkins, is that you?"

"Yes, who am I speaking to?"

"Officer Mayer from last night."

"Is everything okay, Officer Mayer?"

"Did anyone phone you last night?"

"Who do you mean?" I felt icy cold inside. Something was wrong.

"Officer Jack Peters phoned us last night. He said he was going to phone you. I guess he decided to leave it until today."

"Please, you're scaring me. Tell me what's happened." It was the bell that made me jump. I knew it wasn't Sylvie. She had her own front door keys.

"Excuse me, Officer, it's the door. I'll ring you back right away."

Before he had chance to say anything else, I hung up, scared at what he was going to tell me. I stood there at the door, not daring to open it.

"Carla, Carla, it's Jack. Are you there?"

I quickly opened the door, so happy to see him standing there. I heaved a sigh of relief. Everything would be okay. As I looked at his face, my happiness suddenly changed to despair. I could tell that something was on his mind.

"Jack, why are you here? Please don't tell me you've just come to visit, because I won't believe you."

We went into the library as the sitting room had no furniture. I shuddered, afraid of what he might tell me. He was on edge and kept looking around the room, totally ignoring me.

"Jack, just spit it out, please, whatever it may be. I'm a big girl. I can handle anything you have to say to me." I swallowed hard. "You liar," I mumbled quietly to myself so he couldn't hear me.

"Okay. Carla, I am so truly sorry but the police from the Burford Station rang us, Bob Samuels has—"

"Don't." I cut him off before he even had the chance to finish what he was going to say, but I already knew. No words were needed.

"They found him, Carla. I am so truly sorry, but he's dead."

His face looked as solemn as I felt. Tears wanted to fall. I blinked them away, knowing if I started I might never stop. I could feel his hand on mine, then he was holding me in his arms. I just sat there, so close to him with my head on his shoulder, trying to hold back my tears.

He held me so gently in his arms, making me feel

safe. I wanted to stay in his arms forever. As he pulled away from me, all I could see was sheer desire in his eyes and then, without any warning, his lips were on mine.

His kiss sent little shivers down my body. I gently ran my fingertips through his hair as he kissed my neck then my mouth once again, making me giddy with pleasure. I wanted him and I knew he wanted me, but something inside of me told me this was wrong. I didn't want to listen to my mind. As his hand lightly touched my leg, my mind won, and I gently pushed him away. He didn't say anything as I stood up, but I figured he knew what I was thinking.

"Jack, I—"

"You don't have to apologize, Carla, for anything. It's all my fault."

"Jack, I want you but not like this."

"I'm sorry. I should have known better. It won't happen again until you're totally ready."

"Thank you, Jack, thank you."

I went upstairs and freshened up then made Jack a cup of chocolate while I had an orange juice.

"The police found Bob two miles out of Burford in a ditch, naked. His body had been beaten all over with some sort of chain, they think, and there were bite marks all over his face."

As Jack mentioned bite marks, I gasped, shivering all over with fear.

"Carla, what is it?"

"It's them, Jack, they killed him."

"I know."

I was so relieved that Jack had come to the realization that it was them, after all.

Suddenly, I remembered that Sylvie still wasn't back. With everything that had been happening, I had completely forgotten about her, making me feel as guilty as hell. "Jack, I got up today, finding Sylvie out, and I'm really worried something bad has happened to her. It's not like her to go out and not leave some sort of message."

"Have you been in touch with the police down here?"

"No, not about Sylvie. They phoned before you turned up, letting me know you would be in touch, though."

"I'm sure she's okay, probably had to rush off somewhere. She'll be just fine. You wait and see."

I feared the worst, that she was never coming back.

"Don't go upsetting yourself over Sylvie right now, Carla. She'll walk in anytime."

I shrugged, not knowing what to think, but praying he was right.

"I am so sorry about Bob," he said. "I know you liked him very much. I didn't know him, but I do know one thing. He didn't deserve to die."

"Thank you, Jack. I am truly grateful that you're here right now. Don't you dare think of deserting me."

"I won't. I'm right here for you."

I was really worried about Sylvie, especially since she hadn't phoned me at all. I asked Jack to phone around for me, making sure no one else had been found. Everyone he spoke to all said the same thing. No one else had been found. We spent the rest of the morning, ringing around her friends, but no one had seen or heard from her.

I was really scared. My instincts told me she was dead, or else Jake and Will had her alive, hiding her somewhere so she would never be found until they wanted her to be. As I looked at Jack, I knew he was thinking the same as me. I prayed I was wrong.

"Carla, I honestly don't know what to think. I guess it's the waiting game, hoping she will turn up soon."

Waiting for something to happen was like going to the dentist. It was horrible. More than that, I knew it was my fault. If I had never gone camping with my friends that weekend, everyone would still be alive today.

"Stop thinking like that, Carla, you're wrong."

I smiled. He was reading my mind again. "Jack, I— I'm—"

"Shush, darling, the police are doing all they can. They'll find her."

"I can't stop thinking about her, Jack, I'm sorry."

Jack took my hand, leading me to the kitchen, not that I was hungry because right then I wasn't. Sitting there, though, watching him make us scrambled eggs on toast, my stomach started making little groans, letting me know that I was hungrier than I thought. I smiled as he handed me my plate. He would make a great chef if he ever decided to change jobs. After lunch, which went down really well, we went outside into the garden, as it was a lovely warm day. Sitting there on the patio, my mind started to wander.

"What is it, Carla? What were you thinking of right then?"

"Nothing and everything, Jack. Why haven't they phoned? You know who I mean?"

"Yes, I do."

"Well, they haven't phoned once, Jack, but somehow they have found me, haven't they?"

"Why do you say that? Is it because of Sylvie?"

I looked away and didn't answer.

Taking my hand, he gently kissed it. "Please don't be upset."

"Why haven't they phoned me? I guess they don't want to be seen until it's my time."

"You want the truth, kiddo? I don't know why. I honestly have no answers for you."

We sat on the patio for a while in complete silence. Jack still held my hand, making me feel safe, which I was grateful for, as he knew how scared I was. Opening my eyes, I smiled just as he was about to kiss my hand again. As soon as I felt his lips on my hand, giving quick little kisses all over it, I was filled with desire. I thought I had fallen for Will, but being with Jack felt different. It felt totally right. There were no feelings of *This is wrong*, not like when I was with Will. Looking at Jack's beautiful face, I believed we were going to be together forever.

The rest of the day we spent making love. It was wonderful. He was so gentle and loving, giving me goose bumps all over my body. He kept whispering erotic suggestions in my ear, making me laugh. As we lay together, we were one He was part of me, I was part of him. His eyes were aflame with total desire for me. I loved him, wanted him, needed him. We lay totally exhausted in each other's arms, a great big smile on my face. As I looked over at Jack, I saw he had a slight frown on his.

I sat up, turning to look at him. "Was it that bad?"

"Oh, no, my darling,"

Just hearing him call me darling made me go tingly all over.

"It was just that I thought you wanted to wait until everything was over, until you could live a normal life again."

"I know you're right, but I couldn't stop myself."

"Me neither, Carla. I do love you, you know?"

"I love you too and, what the heck? If I'm going to die, I might as well die happy."

"You're not going to die. There will be no more deaths, no more."

I prayed he was right.

We both took a long hot bath together then went downstairs and had an evening snack. I ate it, but wasn't really hungry. All I kept thinking about was Sylvie. I prayed she was alive, but my instincts kept telling me she wasn't.

While I finished in the kitchen, Jack made some more phone calls. But by the look on his face when I went into the library, I knew it wasn't good news.

"Jack, what did they say?"

"The more they search for them, the more they keep coming to a dead end. It's pretty hopeless right now."

"Don't say that. Nothing's hopeless."

"To get them, I guess we're just going to have to wait until they come for you."

"Thanks. I don't like the sound of that."

"Neither do I, princess, neither do I."

"Let's get an early night, shall we?"

As we headed for the stairs, the doorbell rang. I hurried ahead of Jack, relief filling my heart. I knew it was Sylvie. She had most probably just had a day in town and forgot to let me know. God bless her. She must have been in a rush to have forgotten her keys like this.

As I reached the door, I turned and smiled at Jack then slowly opened the front door just as I heard Jack shout "No, Carla, don't open the door."

It was too late. The damage was done. Before I had the chance to shut the door, I felt something slam against my head, then nothing.

CHAPTER 18

I felt numb all over as I started to come around and, as hard as I tried to get up, I couldn't. I knew I must be tied to something as I couldn't move, but feeling so numb and groggy, I couldn't see what. I tried to shout for help, but my mouth was so dry only a croaky sound came out. I sat silently, knowing this was finally it for me, and wondering what had happened to Jack. I prayed he was alive. As I shut my eyes, silently waiting for it to all be over, I heard someone enter the room. Tears slowly slid down my face.

"Hello, Carla girl, we finally meet again. I've missed you, girl, it's been tooo long."

I just sat there staring at Jake, fear curdling my stomach at the sight of this evil monster in front of me.

"Hello, Will me man, here she is."

"Hello, Carla, I knew I would see you again."

I tried to speak. This time my words came out, even though they still sounded a little croaky. "Why? Why are you doing this?"

Before I could say anything else, spit that smelled like rotting flesh hit me in the face, running down my cheeks.

"Why? I'll tell you why, you stupid little bitch. Your father decided to have an affair with my mother. You want to know something else, Carla girl? I killed your father. Yes, it was me. Why, my sweetest one? Because I can."

I didn't believe what Jake had just said. I didn't want to believe it. Tears fell, driven by all the hurt and anger that was inside of me.

"Kill the bitch, kill the stupid bitch, kill her."

I didn't have to see to know who it was. Just by what was said and the sound of her voice I knew. They all stood in front of me. Their faces were ablaze with hatred. My time was up. I tried to move. This time, I could, only slightly, but the numbness was wearing off. Will and Jake stood, staring at me, as the girl walked around the back of me. She had picked up something. I could feel it touching my head. I tried to jerk away but whatever it was that was pressed against my head pressed even harder, making me scream.

"Not yet"

"I want her dead, dead, dead," she spat, sending shivers through my body.

I felt sick to my stomach. If that wasn't bad enough, I could smell the stench coming from her. Urine and faeces, plus pure hatred. It was almost unbearable.

"Where's Jack?" I whispered but, before I could carry on, she was right in front of me, holding a knife against my eye.

I was going to die. Everywhere stank of death.

"Cut it out, cut it out, kill the bitch."

Will looked at Jake then at the girl, then he put his face right next to mine and bit my cheek, just hard enough to make it bleed. Hard enough to hurt. But, for one tiny second, I thought I saw regret in his eyes.

"Where's Jack?"

"Somewhere you will never find him," she hissed at me, drool running down her chin. Then she spat at me, hitting me near my mouth. The stench from her, then from her spit, made me gag then vomit. As I couldn't move, it went down my top and trousers. *Death would be better than this.*

They slowly moved to the back of me so I had no idea where they were. I felt all cold inside. *I don't want to die this way.*

There was complete silence. It was the silence that scared me the most.

I tried to move again, but couldn't. It was then I smelled the rancid stench and heard the heavy breathing coming from somewhere behind me. Suddenly, I felt the worst pain ever. Blood spurted down my neck and my right ear felt like it was on fire. One of them had sliced it with something very sharp. I screamed as the agony began.

CHAPTER 19

I shut my eyes, ready for the worst, when suddenly from a distance I heard a loud bang, then total silence. I knew my time was up so I just sat there, praying it would be quick.

Someone behind me was trying to pull my eyes open just as Jake came and stood a few feet in front of me. My vision was blurred, and I was in agony from all of my injuries. I wondered what I had ever seen in him, then I remembered that I had never known him, only his brother. But this twin reminded me of a picture I had seen of the Devil.

"Carla girl, you're going to die, you little slut. You're—"

He didn't get the chance to say anything else as a

gun went off, the bullet hitting him right between his eyes. I heard a scream and another gunshot. Someone fell to the floor behind me. Then I felt a blade against my neck. I knew if I tried moving, it would cut me, so I just shut my eyes again and waited.

"Put the knife down and move away."

"I'll kill the bitch," she screamed.

"Put the knife down."

I couldn't see whoever it was, as they were behind me. Was I finally safe? Then I looked upward, screaming as the blade came toward my eyes. Another gunshot sounded and she fell to the ground.

"Carla, Carla sweetheart, are you all right?"

I smiled as I saw his handsome face. He was alive. I thanked God that he was alive.

"Carla, I love you," Jack whispered to me as he cut my restraints.

He was covered in bruises with blood on his shirt, but he still could smile after telling me all that had happened. He'd been beaten and tied up, but somehow he'd managed to get free when they left him alone to torment me. He'd left his gun upstairs in the bedroom, and he'd had to sneak up there and retrieve it before he could rescue me. Now, he held me gently in his arms.

"Jack, why did you shout at the last minute?"

"I suddenly realized the danger you could be in. I knew Mrs. Dorson would have let herself in, so if it wasn't her, it was most likely Jake, but I was too late. You had already opened the door."

I nodded. "He said that my father had an affair with his mother and he'd killed my father. If it's true, I know nothing about it." I didn't know what to think. Maybe I should just leave the past in the past. "Who was Will?"

"Like I said, we don't really know, but we gather he had known Jake a long time, and Will had been helping him. That's how he knew where to find you."

I shuddered, feeling sick inside, but glad to be alive.

"Sylvie! Where is she? Have they found her? I—"

He gently touched my face, his eyes full of love for me, as he pulled out his cell phone. He talked for a few minutes then hung up.

"Did they find her?" I asked. "Is she—"

"Hush, my darling, she's safe. The police found her. She's going to be all right. She's been taken to the Huntingdon Hospital in Chingford. They found her in the park, tied up, but just a few cuts and bruises. I'll drive you to see her. She's been asking for you, so I've been told."

As he held me in his arms, I realized things would never be the same again. No, they would be better. The nightmare was finally over, and a new beginning was about to start.

THE END

About the Author

One of eleven children, and with a twin sister, Carrie Quesne was born and raised in Peterborough, England, and soon after moved with her family to the iconic sea-side town of Brighton.

Ever since childhood, she has always had a vivid, flya-way imagination and not quite known what to do with it. What ignites her imagination the most is her love of hor-ror movies, which she stumbled across in her early teens.

Quesne would say that her passion for writing began at school when she first allowed her imagination to take form on paper. It is only now that she has truly decided to take the leap into publishing her stories.

Amongst many others, Quesne counts James Herbert, Pe-ter James, Stephen King, and Clive James as some of her all-time favourite authors and hopes to follow in their footsteps in creating dramatic, thought-provoking stories.

When she doesn't have her head in a book, she counts baking as her favorite hobby and often bakes for her ex-tremely large extended family.